REVENGE

OF THE TEACHER'S PETS

Don't miss any adventures with The Brewster Triplets!

Revenge of the Flower Girls
Revenge of the Angels
Revenge of the Happy Campers

REVENGE
OF THE TEACHER'S PETS

JENNIFER ZIEGLER

SCHOLASTIC INC.

10 9 8 7 6 5 4 3 2 1   18 19 20 21 22 • Printed in the U.S.A. 40 • First printing 2018
Book design by Yaffa Jaskoll

TO MOM,
MY FIRST AND BEST TEACHER

CHAPTER ONE

Old Glory

Darby

It was all our faults that we turned into troublemakers in seventh grade. Before school started, everything was fine. In fact, we'd just had our best summer yet. Here is the evidence:

- Our older sister, Lily, and her fiancé, Alex, both graduated from college and moved back to town. Plus, Aunt Jane, who had been living in Boston since we were four, sold her pub and moved back to Texas. Now she was helping to run a campground that's a few hours from here. Everyone we loved was back in Texas.

- Lily and Alex were finally going to get married! They were probably going to hold the wedding over Thanksgiving break, since everyone would have time off — and because that's Lily's favorite holiday. In the meantime, Alex was working for a Texas congress-woman, and Lily had taken a part-time job at the library here in Johnson City and was living at home with us.

- We grew almost two inches! Delaney was still the tallest by about a quarter of an inch, followed by Dawn, then me. (Although I think Dawn might have cheated a little and puffed herself up when we got measured.)

- We got lasso lessons from Lucas Westbrook. We also had lots of fun on the Slip 'n' Slide down the hill behind our house, and at Lake Lewis, the campground where Aunt Jane was now working. Plus, altogether we read twenty-four books and each earned a free ice-cream cone.

But on the last day of vacation, everything started going bad . . .

I sat on the porch swing, yawning and trying to blink my eyes wider and wider. We'd woken up early to hang our American flag and do back-to-school exercises. Dawn and I had gotten used to sleeping late over the summer and needed to get back into the habit of waking up at 6:45 a.m. Since Delaney always gets up early, no matter what time of year, she didn't need to practice. Instead, she was working on something else.

"Delaney, your foot keeps bouncing," Dawn said. "You're shaking the swing."

"I'm being still and quiet!" Delaney said. She was sitting on my right at one end of the porch swing. Her back was so stiff and straight, she wasn't even resting against the back slats. And Dawn was right — Delaney was wiggling her feet so much, the whole swing jostled.

"When we said practice sitting quietly, we didn't mean like a statue," Dawn said. She was on my left, at the other end of the swing, which meant I was stuck in the middle. Since I was born in the middle, I was sort of used to it.

"It's the only thing that works," Delaney said. "If I make myself super still, I won't wiggle."

"Well, your feet aren't getting the message," Dawn grouched.

"I'm doing my best!" Delaney said.

"She's trying," I repeated. I knew that Delaney usually spent her mornings bouncing in the yard with Mynah, her pet rabbit, or playing chase with Quincy, our loyal yellow Labrador, to get out all her pent-up energy. But since she hadn't done either of those things yet, she was extra wiggly. "I think we should be more supportive."

Dawn made a harrumphing noise. Probably because she knew I was right but didn't want to admit it. Dawn felt she was our leader — and not just because she was born first.

She is just one of those strong-willed types who can't help taking charge. Of everyone. All the time.

I yawned again and gazed up at our flag, waving in the breeze atop the pole in our front yard. I love how the wind makes flags dance and flap — or, if there's no wind, sag as if they feel sulky. It's like they can go through different moods or get tired or excited, just like people. I guess that's why they're such good symbols for nations. Nations are full of people.

I felt a little bit of shaking and glanced over at Delaney. She wasn't jiggling her legs, but her rear end must have been shimmying ever so slightly, enough to make the swing move.

"Don't worry, Delaney," I said, patting her left shoulder. "Just ten more minutes and we'll have flag marching practice."

That made Delaney smile without turning her head. The best thing about going into seventh grade was that we could now be in the Color Guard, a special troop that officially hangs the school's American flag every morning. The group also marches and does routines at football games and other special events with silver and navy flags, our school colors. Almost every day this summer, after hanging our own flag, we'd rehearse twirling and marching with our old Quidditch broomsticks so that we'd be the best in the regiment.

In elementary school, we'd helped raise the flag every morning on account of our extensive knowledge about how to correctly handle the Stars and Stripes. When we went to middle school, we were told that the Color Guard did that as part of their duties, but only seventh and eighth graders could be in it. So really, we've been waiting for over a year, not just a summer. We were eager to go back to official flag duties. At our old school, we'd been known as the expert flag girls, and it was nice. It made us feel important.

Unfortunately, mentioning flag practice made Delaney excited, and her feet started kicking again.

"Stop bouncing the swing!" Dawn said.

"Sorry." Delaney's forehead scrunched in a look of intense concentration — or maybe pain.

I felt bad for her. "You know, Dawn," I said, "you should work on not being so high-handed."

"I'm not being high-handed."

"You are," Delaney said, nodding her head ever so slightly while still staring straight ahead. "And quarrelsome."

"I'm not —" Dawn stopped herself. She pursed her lips together and folded her arms across her chest, as if she were trying to trap her words inside of her.

"You should practice not being that way. School isn't the place to be telling people what to do all the time," Delaney said.

"Sure it is. If you remember, I was an exemplary hall monitor in fifth grade." Dawn lifted her chin proudly.

"Yeah, except that our school didn't actually have hall monitors," I pointed out. "But you made yourself one anyway."

"Oh, right." Dawn's eyes swiveled upward. "I forgot."

I chuckled to myself, remembering how Dawn would hand out hallway warnings that she'd made herself out of Mom's yellow sticky pads. The students were confused, but they actually did what she said. I guess they'd assumed she was official. She probably would have gotten away with it a lot longer if she hadn't given a warning to Ms. Mendoza, the school clerk, when she was running down the hall to answer the office phone. Sometimes Dawn can get a little carried away.

When I laughed at the memory, Dawn must have thought I was making fun of her, because she scowled at me. "You also need to work on something else, Darby," she said. "You need to practice not being so bashful."

It was my turn to scowl. I knew Dawn was just trying to get back at me, but she was also right. I'm shy around people I don't know very well, so school can be kind of frightful. Luckily, I have two loudmouthed sisters who will speak up for me.

"Oh, hey. Here comes Mr. Pete with the mail," Dawn said, pointing toward the white post office truck that was stopping at mailboxes next to all the driveways on our street. "Darby, maybe you should —"

"I'll get it!" Delaney shouted, leaping off the swing. Before we could say anything more, she was racing up the driveway. The dust churned up by her sneakers made it seem like she was leaving a trail of exhaust smoke.

"Dadgummit," Dawn grumbled, "I wanted you to do it. Seriously, Darby, your training should be to talk to someone outside of close friends and family."

"I could go over and visit with Ms. Woolcott." I pointed toward our next-door neighbor's house.

"No," Dawn said. "I don't think that's the best solution. You already know Ms. Woolcott pretty well. Besides, she'd do all the talking."

I nodded. Ms. Woolcott sure loved to chat.

"I know!" Dawn suddenly sat up as straight as Delaney had been. "You should walk down the road and introduce yourself to the new neighbors."

My face went tingly. "But . . . why?"

"Because it's what decent folk do. Besides, I heard they have a kid our age."

I'd heard that, too. Ms. Woolcott had told us that a few days ago, when we were talking with her by the fence. Unlike me, Ms. Woolcott had done her best to find out everything about the people who moved into the brown house with the giant live oak out front — the one that used to belong to Mr. Hockley, the high school basketball coach, before he retired and moved someplace that had better fishing. (That's another one of the things Ms. Woolcott told us.)

"Face it," Dawn went on. "You've got to stop being so chicken-hearted around people, and this would be the best way to practice."

I glanced over at Delaney, who was still standing at the

end of our drive, chatting with Mr. Pete. Some poor towns-folk would get their mail late today.

I felt a twinge of envy. If only I could be a little more like Delaney. She could talk to anyone at any time.

"In solidarity with you, I promise to do my darndest not to ride herd over folks." Dawn tilted her head and her fore-head went wavy. She seemed sincere. "Deal?"

"Deal," I said and then held out my hand for her to shake. But before she could, we heard a commotion in the distance.

"Emergency!" Delaney was running down the driveway toward us, shouting and waving some papers in her right hand. "Emergency! Emergency!"

Dawn and I exchanged confused looks and ran to the porch railing. It didn't seem like there was an emergency. There was no wreckage on the road behind her and Delaney didn't look injured.

"Ding-dang it, Delaney," Dawn said. "What's all the hol-lering about? You're going to get the cops called on us again."

Delaney came to a stop right in front of us, but kept bouncing on her toes as if she wanted to still be running. Her forehead was all crisscrossed with worry. "We got our school schedules in the mail," she said, lifting her hand with the papers in them, "and they're all messed up!"

"How do you know?" I asked.

Delaney paused and bit her lip. "Because I accidentally looked at everyone's schedules after I opened the envelopes."

She handed each of us a paper with our name at the top. "See?" she said, holding hers up and pointing. "We don't have any classes together except one."

It took me a while to find what she was talking about. My gaze hopped from my paper to the other two schedules, checking to see if any of the same classes were listed on all of them. Dawn saw it before I did.

"What in the blazes?" she exclaimed. "Cheer Squad?"

That's when my eyes found it. Sure enough, all three of us were taking Cheer Squad at sixth period, the last class of the day.

"But . . . where's Color Guard?" I asked.

"It's not on there," Delaney said. "It's not on any of our schedules."

Hardly any classes together? No Color Guard? I felt a swoopy sensation, as if I were still on the swing.

"You're right, Delaney." Dawn's steely-eyed expression returned to her face. "This is an emergency."

CHAPTER TWO

Political Office

Delaney

We stormed into the house and found Mom and Lily sitting at the breakfast table. Mom was in her bathrobe holding a coffee cup, and her face looked as droopy-tired as Dawn's and Darby's usually do in the mornings. Meanwhile, Lily was all dressed up for work in a white blouse and a peach-colored flowery skirt. She seemed bright-eyed and alert as she ate her yogurt. Lily is like me and wants to get moving as soon as she wakes up. But unfortunately she never has time for cartwheels and bouncing in the yard.

As soon as we burst through the door, yelling, "Emergency!" they jumped up from their seats, looking worried.

"What's going on?" Lily asked. "What emergency?"

"They put us in the wrong class!" Dawn said.

"We aren't in Color Guard!" Darby said.

"We won't see each other all day except for the wrong class!" I said.

Mom told us to calm down and had us explain a little more. Once she understood what had happened, she told us not to fret. She pointed to some small type at the bottom of the page. "See?" she said. "It says here to contact your counselor, Avery Plunkett, in case of questions or problems."

"Or emergencies?" I asked.

"That, too, probably," she said.

"Then let's go!" Dawn said. "Time is of the essence!"

"I'm not ready just yet," Mom said, gesturing to her fluffy bathrobe. "I can take you later."

"But how much later?" Darby asked. Her voice was all wobbly.

"Who says you have to change? Bathrobes shouldn't matter when it's an emergency," I said.

"Besides, we won't be able to do anything else until we get this fixed. We'll be all fretful and in your hair. Delaney's already in a tizzy," Dawn said.

I had started pacing in circles, as I usually do when I'm upset. I would have jogged, but I'm not supposed to do that indoors. Besides, there was no room with five of us and our big dog all jammed in our small kitchen.

Unfortunately, our whining didn't seem to be working. Mom wasn't moving any faster. In fact, she looked even more tired. "How about you girls walk?" Mom suggested. "After all, you walk to and from school when it's in session."

"But this is a crisis of epic proportions!" Dawn said, waving her arms wildly. "Every second counts!"

"How about I take them on my way to work?" Lily said.

Mom said thank you to Lily and told the three of us to walk home as soon as it was done, or call her from the office phone for a ride. We let Lily take a couple more bites of yogurt and then we all headed out to her car. Since Dawn, Darby, and I were in such a nervous fluster, none of us called shotgun. Instead, all three of us climbed into the backseat, with me in the middle, and no one sat in the passenger seat next to Lily.

"Do you really think Mr. Plunkett can fix this?" Darby asked as we headed down Nugent Avenue. She had worried eyes — big and round and kind of saggy in the corners.

I put my hand on her shoulder. "Probably all we have to do is point out the blunder to him," I said. "I'm sure it's only a misunderstanding."

"It better be," Dawn said. Her eyes, unlike Darby's, were grouchy.

"Dawn," Lily said. She also caught Dawn's eyes in the rearview mirror. "You know, you'll get much better results if you remain polite and diplomatic. You want to show them how mature you are — that you're the kind of students who should be allowed in Color Guard."

Lily was eleven years old when we were born, so she's kind of like another parent to us — but the kind that lets you get four cookies instead of three and cries in the theater with you when the movie is sad. Plus, she's real good at scolding us without making it seem like she's scolding.

"I promise we'll be polite," Dawn said.

"Good."

Soon Lily was pulling into the parking lot of our middle school. "Head on home when you're done so Mom won't worry. Or call her," she said. "And good luck!"

We thanked Lily, jumped out of the car, and marched toward the entrance. Dawn was leading the way with that purposeful firstborn stride of hers, while Darby and I lagged behind, glancing around at the familiar surroundings. Schools always look so different when it's summertime. Kind of deserted and lonely, like an empty piecrust. I said this to Darby and she agreed. "The school will be happier when we're all back," she said, and patted the flagpole as we went past.

"It's probably best if I do the talking," Dawn told us as we pushed through the doors and walked down the corridor toward the main office.

"Do we have a plan?" I asked her.

"It should be simple," she said. "We'll just show them the evidence and they'll admit they messed up. Then we graciously accept their apology and move on."

We weren't the first ones there. Two other kids were already sitting with their parents in chairs lined up in the hallway. Keeping Lily's advice in mind, we took three seats and waited patiently. Well, at least Dawn and Darby did. After a couple of moments, I didn't want to sit any longer and started wandering the halls, trying to peek into the dark classrooms. I spied Mrs. Gillespie, my science teacher from last year, setting up a bulletin board in her room, and Mr. Langerham, my old math teacher, organizing his supply cabinet. It's funny seeing teachers in shorts and T-shirts. There's just something wrong about it — like having the president of the United States make a speech in pajamas. Eventually I heard Dawn calling out for me, and it was our turn to meet with the counselor.

Mr. Plunkett was about our dad's age. Unlike our dad, he had hair on the top of his head and wore gold wire-rimmed glasses that he was always taking off and putting back on.

I couldn't say that we liked Mr. Plunkett, but we didn't dislike him, either. We knew he was important in the school, but thought about him the same way we thought about the doorknobs — by which I mean hardly ever. Plus, Mr. Plunkett had one of those blank faces that didn't really smile or frown, so it was hard to know what to make of him.

When we walked into his office, he turned away from his computer and looked at the three of us standing in a row on the other side of his desk.

"How can I help you?" he asked, taking off his glasses.

Darby and I glanced over at Dawn. She's almost always the one who talks to the grown-ups for us. Mainly because she thinks she is one.

"Hello. We're Dawn, Darby, and Delaney Brewster. Thank you for seeing us," she said. Her voice was all sticky-sweet, like the lady on the Honeysuckle Honey commercial.

"Yes? What seems to be the matter?" Mr. Plunkett asked.

"Uh . . . well . . ." Dawn cleared her throat and took a deep breath. I could tell she was trying hard not to get riled. "We received our schedules in the mail today, and it appears that they are all . . . botched up."

Mr. Plunkett's eyebrows rose up under his hair. "How so?"

"Well, first off, we always have most of our classes together. That's how it's always been, and that's how we like it. But for some reason, that's not the case this time. This year we're all separated."

"That is true," he said, nodding.

Dawn tilted her head. "You know about this?"

"Yes, I was the one who created your schedules."

"Well then." Dawn seemed confused. "I do appreciate your coming right out and admitting your mistake, but if you could just —"

"There was no mistake," he said.

Dawn, Darby, and I traded shocked glances.

"But why?" I asked him. "Why would you want to bust up a happy family?"

Mr. Plunkett put his glasses back on. "I am not trying to hurt your family, I assure you. Studies show that siblings do best when they are separated. Our school was too small and just didn't have enough teachers to put all three of you in different classes. But this year we've expanded enough that we can."

"But we've been doing great so far." Dawn opened her

arms to gesture at all three of us. "Look at the results. We're highly intelligent, responsible, and . . . and . . ."

"Polite," Darby added.

"And clean," I added.

"Yes," Mr. Plunkett said. "You three are model students."

"Then why separate us? Why mess with something that isn't broken?" Dawn's talking was high and fast, like a squirrel's. She seemed to realize she was losing her grown-up disguise and paused to take a breath. "The thing is," she added more calmly, "we just always go together. Like a team."

"I understand," Mr. Plunkett said. I thought he might bristle at Dawn's complaining, but he didn't sound upset at all. In fact, his face looked softer — as if he were smiling without a smile. "However, I'm afraid that the decision has been made," he went on, "and I think you three should give it an honest try. If by midyear you still feel it's a big mistake, we can meet and discuss other options. But give it a chance. That's fair of us to ask, isn't it?"

Darby nodded sadly. She's all about being fair — even if it means we don't get our way. It can be annoying, but it's also what will make her a great chief justice of the Supreme Court someday. Dawn scowled, but didn't say anything further. I think she knew Mr. Plunkett was being reasonable and felt she couldn't argue with him. Or she hadn't thought of a good opposing theory yet.

Meanwhile I just wiggled my toes nervously inside my sneakers. Even though I thought he was making a good point, it was still weird and scary to think of us being in different classes all day long.

"Well then, it sounds like we have an agreement." This time, an actual smile appeared on Mr. Plunkett's face.

"I guess. For now anyway," Dawn said with an exasperated sigh. "But we've got another problem. You put us in Cheer Squad when we didn't even sign up for it." She held up our schedules in her right hand.

"It's true," Darby said in a quiet voice. "We signed up for Color Guard."

"Yeah!" I said, bouncing even higher on my toes. "We've been practicing and practicing. We're probably the best ones. Only now we aren't even going to be doing it. It's a tragedy for the whole school."

Mr. Plunkett was the one to look confused. "Let me see those." He reached for our schedules and, after glancing at them, typed on his computer for a bit. Then he pulled a light green paper out of a drawer, ran his finger down the middle of it, and set it down on his desk near us. "See here?" he said, tapping the page with his fingertip. "This is a sign-up sheet for the class. And those are your names, right?"

We all gathered around the paper. Sure enough, our names were there, all in a row. At the very top of the page was a bit of small text:

Want to lead the Patriots to victory and boost school spirit?

Sign up today to be on Cheer Squad!

"Wait a minute," Dawn said. "How did our names get on the Cheer Squad sheet without us realizing it?"

Darby shrugged.

I stared hard at the celery-colored form. Something about it seemed familiar. I closed my eyes and tried to remember . . . Suddenly it came to me.

"Corny dogs!" I cried. "Remember the last day of sixth grade when they had the booster festival on the school lawn and we wanted corn dogs?"

Dawn frowned. "Delaney, you're making no sense. What does that have to do with our schedules?"

"They had a sign-up sheet at the table with the corn dogs. I figured you had to sign if you wanted to eat, so I added all our names."

"Can I see that, please?" Dawn reached for the paper and Mr. Plunkett handed it over. Darby and I leaned in to examine it. "That's Delaney's handwriting, all right. Well, what do you know? Foiled by our own sister."

"I'm sorry! I was hungry and didn't read the fine print."

"So . . . we actually *did* register for Cheer Squad?" Darby mumbled.

Mr. Plunkett took his glasses off and started cleaning

them. "I'm afraid so," he said, nodding. "In fact, Delaney signed twice."

I thought for a moment. "Oh yeah. I went back for second corn dog."

"But it's trickery!" Dawn's honey voice was gone. Now she was in full-on angry squirrel mode. "Those charlatans lured us with deep-fried goodness! Isn't that grounds for a schedule change?"

"I understand it was unintentional, but Color Guard is completely full. I could get you into other elective classes, though." Mr. Plunkett put his glasses back on and started typing at the computer again. "Let's see . . . One of you could join choir, another could . . ."

"Can't you put all three of us into another class?" I asked.

"Sorry," he said, glancing back up at us. He really did look sorry. "None of them have three openings, so I'm afraid not."

"What do we do now?" Darby asked, turning about to face Dawn and me.

"Cheer Squad is the only class we have together," I pointed out.

Dawn scowled. "I don't want to take Cheer Squad, but I like the idea of us having zero classes together even less."

"Same here," I said.

Darby nodded.

"I guess it's unanimous." Dawn looked defeated — a rare and worrisome sight. "Mr. Plunkett, we've officially voted to stay in Cheer Squad until you can get all of us into Color

Guard. Although I will be checking with you pretty regularly to see if there are any changes."

"I understand, and I admire you girls for being willing to give it a try." Mr. Plunkett did that thing again where his eyes smiled even though his mouth didn't. "I feel confident that each of you will do well regardless. And remember, if you ever want to come by and talk to me about this, my door is always open."

"You might need to get another chair," I said, glancing around.

"No, I meant *you* in the singular. I would want to talk with you one-on-one."

I noticed the perplexed looks on Dawn's and Darby's faces and knew they felt the same way I did — that the thought of having a meeting without our other sisters around was too weird to comprehend. Why was the school so determined to break us up?

"Thanks for being open-minded." Mr. Plunkett put his glasses back on. "I have other students to see, so let's end it here."

We mumbled our sad-sounding good-byes and filed out of his office, all slumpy and defeated.

"This is not how I thought our seventh grade would start," I grumbled as we trudged down the echoey hallway toward the exit.

"Me either," Dawn said.

WE MUST
NEVER BE
AFRAID TO
GO TOO FAR,
FOR TRUTH
LIES BEYOND.

MARCEL PROUST

TRUTH

ASK YOURSELF:
AM I BEING...

HONEST?

REAL?

OPEN?

MEANINGFUL?

UNDERSTANDING?

HELPFUL?

"At least we tried our best," Darby said. "We just have to accept it and move on."

"Maybe not." Dawn stopped in the middle of the corridor and gazed into the distance.

I recognized the expression on her face. That ten-mile stare . . . Her eyebrows pushing together over her nose . . . Her index finger tapping against the side of her chin . . . Yep, she was formulating plans, all right. And her plans usually involved all three of us — and possibly shenanigans.

Summer fun was officially over.

CHAPTER THREE

Declaration

Dawn

For the last time" — Mom sighed, her eyes closed, and rubbed the bridge of her nose — "I am *not* hiring a lawyer."

We were starting our second hour of discussion after she'd picked us up from school. I knew she had work to do, and I knew I should go eat my grilled cheese sandwich, even though it had gone cold on the kitchen table. Darby and Delaney had already eaten their lunch and wandered off to do other things. Darby was upstairs, probably reading, and I occasionally caught glimpses of Delaney through the window, bouncing and playing with Mynah. Meanwhile, I was still arguing our case, determined to get Mom to see things my way. For some reason, though, she was being stubborn.

"But, Mom! It's wrong what they're doing to us. It's tyrannical! It's undemocratic!"

"Schools are not democracies."

"Why not? They're part of a democracy, so everyone

there should get a say in what happens to them. There should be checks and balances and clear paths to justice. No taxation without representation! Or . . . no surprise schedule changes."

Mom just looked at me. Her eyes were more weary-looking than angry. After a long moment, she reached out and gave me a big hug. It was both nice and confusing. I don't know why, but tears came to my eyes. Not that I was crying — I wasn't.

As she held me, Mom said, "I can't help you with this one, Dawn. I'm sorry." Then she let go and took a step back, again fixing me with that hard-to-read expression. "It's not that I don't want to, it's that I can't. But also, I have to say on the record, I don't think this is a bad thing. You three can't always do everything together."

"Of course we can," I grumbled. "Why not?"

Mom reached out and brushed my hair away from my face. "Because that's not how the world works. That's not even how democracies work. Please try to accept it. Try to give this new schedule a chance."

She was wrong. Mr. Plunkett was wrong. The whole school system was wrong! My sisters and I needed each other. The Brewster triplets were one for all and all for one, and we fought together for truth, justice, and the American way. Busting up our union would be like dividing the country. We just wouldn't be as good — or as powerful — on our own. And yet everyone refused to acknowledge this.

More wetness came into my eyes; it still wasn't tears, though. I was just surprised and disappointed that our own mom was siding with the enemy.

Over her shoulder, I could see a framed photo on her desk — Mom sitting on the porch swing with Delaney and me on either side of her and Darby on her lap. It was from only about three years ago, but I was surprised at how much we'd grown since then. I couldn't remember the last time I'd sat on Mom's lap, or Dad's. Why did everything feel so different all of a sudden?

I pursed my lips together and tried to bully the frustration-wetness back into my ducts. Only it didn't work. Just as the drops came rolling down, I turned and stomped out of there.

"I call this emergency meeting to order," I said, pounding my fist on my wooden headboard.

After I got nowhere with Mom, I rounded everyone up for some official business in the Triangular Office, which is what we call our attic bedroom. I balanced cross-legged on my bed, Delaney sat — or rather, bounced — on her bed, and Darby took her usual spot at the desk we shared, so she could type up the official minutes.

"Our situation is dire," I went on. "Mom has turned traitor and refused to help, no matter how hard I tried to make her see the light. And I want it officially noted that I was by myself in those efforts."

Darby stopped typing and looked at me. "Hey, we tried for the first half hour."

"After she said no for the twelfth time, I figured she meant no and went outside," Delaney said with a shrug.

"The point is," I said kind of loudly, "we're on our own — at least for now. When Dad gets back in town, we'll see where he stands on all this. Until then, it's up to us."

"But what can we do? Tomorrow is the first day of school." Delaney was bouncing higher and higher, making her voice all quivery.

I tapped my finger against my chin. "I know! We could write letters to the superintendent and the school board."

"Yeah, but . . . remember? They stopped answering our letters," Delaney said. "We haven't gotten a response from them in, like, two years."

"Then we go to the press! The local paper would be interested in knowing that three honor students are being picked on by the establishment."

"Um . . . won't we need some sort of evidence of wrongdoing?" Darby asked. "The only documentation that exists is a green piece of paper we signed. One of us, anyway."

"Plus, we already ate the corn dogs," Delaney said. "That evidence is gone."

I shut my eyes and leaned my head back against the wall, waiting for one of my brilliant ideas to pop into my brain — but nothing came. "You're right," I said finally. "I hate to say it, but we're going to have to go into stealth mode. Watch, wait, and learn. Spy if you have to. And we need allies, so see if you can turn any powerful people against the school."

Darby and Delaney exchanged nervous glances.

"But also," I added, "be model students. We can't start even a hint of trouble because we have to prove that we deserve Color Guard — and to be in the same classes together."

I waited for them to reply, but they just sat there, glum as mud. Delaney had even stopped bouncing.

"Come on, troops. This is our call to arms, our finest hour. It could be the worst thing we've ever faced." I hopped off my bed and stood before them, hands on hips. "But we'll be ready. The school, the town — heck, the whole world — will know better than to mess with the Brewster triplets again."

CHAPTER FOUR

Inauguration

Darby

On the first day of school there were butterflies in my stomach. Actually, they felt less like butterflies and more like giant winged creatures. Bald eagles, maybe?

We stood in the school foyer not saying anything. All around us kids were walking past, clutching their schedules. In some ways, it was just like any other first day of school. Everyone had on new-looking backpacks and their best clothes. School supplies were neat and colorful, the walls and floors were shiny clean, and the teachers were actually smiling. But this day was different.

This day we wouldn't march down the hall as a unit as we usually did, with Delaney slightly in front and me slightly in back and Dawn in the middle. We wouldn't hold brief meetings to decide where to sit in class. We wouldn't say the Pledge of Allegiance together, our three voices combining to be the loudest and proudest in the class — maybe even the whole school.

Nope. Instead of heading off to our first class together, Dawn would go to the science wing, Delaney would skip off to her Spanish class, and I would search for room 207 to take Mrs. Champion's history class.

"Mrs. Champion is a great name," Delaney said when she noticed my face. I was trying not to have big scared eyes or worry squiggles on my forehead, but when you're a triplet, it's just not possible to fool your sisters.

"Yeah, it's a good sign," Dawn said, patting my shoulder. "You'll do great."

I nodded and tried to look brave. Just then the warning bell rang. We had five minutes to get to class or we'd get marked tardy.

"Okay, there's the bell! Gotta go! Bye!" Delaney said, and raced off toward the north hallway.

"Good luck," Dawn said. She gave me a reassuring smile and headed down the center hallway where all the science labs were.

"Bye," I said — only no sound came out. Just air.

Everyone was rushing all around while I stayed in place, like I was in slow motion and they were in fast motion. It reminded me of when I was learning to go off the high dive at the local pool. I had the same twisty feeling in my stomach — part excitement and part terror — and the same awareness that I was being watched. I knew I had to muster my nerve, take a deep breath, and . . . leap. *Just get through the first day*, I told myself. *It will all get better after that. And remember — you love the high dive now.*

Closing my eyes, I summoned my strength and forced my feet to start walking. Luckily I reopened my eyes before I banged into a locker.

Room 207 was at the end of the main hallway. It was pretty far to go by myself. Not treacherous or anything, but a long time to feel scared and lonely. On the way, a few people I knew said hi to me. I waved back at them, since my voice was still hiding.

Mrs. Champion was standing by the door when I came in. "Good morning," she said, smiling. "Sit wherever you like." She seemed young — maybe just a few years older than Lily — with green eyes and shoulder-length hair the color of a lucky penny. Like Lily, she had a really friendly smile. It made the squeezy sensation in my chest feel better.

As I came farther into the room, I stopped in surprise. The desks weren't in rows, like in all the other classes I've had in middle school. Instead, they were in an oval shape, and her desk was part of the circle, too. I didn't know what to do. I'd been hoping to find a spot where I could hide — not too far in back, but not in the front. Best of all would be in the middle, behind a really tall person.

The eagles in my stomach were starting to flap again.

Everyone was moving around and talking, so I couldn't even figure out where to sit. It made me feel kind of invisible.

Then I noticed someone looking at me. A girl was sitting at one of the desks. I'd never seen her before, but I liked that she was sitting quietly. I also liked her hair. It was dark brown, almost black, and cut so it was short in the back and long in the front — so long in the front that I couldn't even see her eyes clearly. I wished I had hair I could hide behind.

I plopped into the chair to the girl's left, farther away from the teacher's desk, and started unpacking my backpack. I felt like I should say hi, but I was still too nervous to talk. So I pretended I couldn't find my pen, even though it was right there in the pocket.

As I rummaged around, I noticed that Tucker Burnett was sitting at the desk on the other side of me. He's one of those kids who always lets out loud sighs when the teacher assigns work. At track and field day last spring, Tucker wouldn't take his baseball cap off during "The Star-Spangled Banner," and Dawn lit into him with a tirade about patriotism and respect.

Today he wasn't wearing a cap, but he was chewing gum, which was against the rules. He frowned at me when he saw me looking at him and turned the other way.

Eventually I had all my supplies out on the table and sat waiting for the teacher to start. When I glanced in the direction of Mrs. Champion's desk, I could see that the girl was looking at me. At least I'm pretty sure she was. Her head was angled just right and there was a glimmer of her eyes behind her bangs. It made me feel shy and I wanted to turn away, but then I thought it would make me look rude like Tucker.

Luckily, right at that moment, the bell rang and Mrs. Champion started clapping her hands together. "All right. Quiet down, everyone. I'm passing around a seating chart and I want each of you to write your name on the square that represents your desk. Unless I tell you otherwise, this is where you will sit every day."

I focused on rolling my pen back and forth while I waited for the form. Soon the girl handed it to me, and I saw the name she'd neatly printed on the square that represented her desk:

Wanda Vasquez

She grinned at me. I thought perhaps I should say something, but what? It seemed too late for hi, and the only other thing I could think of was "I like your hair" — which sounded silly, even in my head.

After carefully checking that there wasn't any fine print anywhere, I wrote my name neatly inside my square and passed the paper along to Tucker. When he saw my name, he heaved a big sigh. "Oh, good. I thought you were Dawn."

I ignored him and glanced around the room instead. I

find that you can tell a lot about teachers by the things they hang on the wall and how messy their desks are. Mrs. Champion's desk was really tidy, except for a stack of newspapers. Taped up all over the room were posters of things I recognized: a laminated Bill of Rights, a big map of Texas, a photo of Martin Luther King Jr. waving to a large crowd, and (my favorite) a copy of the famous Rosie the Riveter poster, with *We Can Do It!* printed above her as she flexes her bicep. I started to feel better about being there.

Mrs. Champion had gotten the seating chart back and was now standing inside the circle of desks. Just as she opened her mouth to say something, we heard the pops and crackles of the intercom overhead. "Good morning, students, and welcome to another great year at Johnson City Middle School," came the voice of our principal, Mrs. Jessup. "Would y'all please stand for the Pledge of Allegiance?"

Suddenly everyone was on their feet and facing me. I gulped. That was when I realized the flag was on the wall directly over my head. I turned to look at it, but somehow I could still sense everyone's eyes — like two dozen mosquitoes biting me at the same time. I wished I'd chosen a different desk, but now that I was on the chart, it was probably permanent. Because I was so nervous, and because my sisters weren't there with me, I didn't say the Pledge loud and proud like I usually do. This made me feel kind of guilty, but I'm pretty sure it still counted.

Finally we were all sitting back down and Mrs. Champion introduced herself. She stood in the middle of the oval and walked in a slow circle as she talked, making eye contact with each of us.

"I want you to know that my class is a little different from other classes," she said. "I feel that you are all old enough to understand what's going on in the world and have opinions about it. That's why we won't just be using textbooks and worksheets. We'll also be reading newspapers and discussing current events and making connections. Because history isn't just the past — it's happening all the time, all around us."

I grinned and sat up straight so she could see me smile at her. I wanted her to know that I understood what she said and agreed with her. I wanted her to see that, even though lots of other seventh graders didn't seem to care about history, I did. And I realized that this could end up being my very favorite class — even without my sisters around.

"Also," she went on, "unlike other classes, I allow talking. In fact, I demand it."

Now other students were sitting up and smiling. I heard Tucker mutter, "All right."

Mrs. Champion paused and smiled. "Allow me to explain," she said. "Every class will have time devoted to discussing topics and sharing our ideas and experiences. Part of learning — in fact, part of democracy — is participation, so I am requiring all of you to contribute to the conversation. One third of your grade depends on it."

As she spoke, I could feel myself slowly slipping down in my chair until just my nose and eyes were peeking up over the table. It looked like this wouldn't be my favorite class after all. Now I wasn't just worried about getting through the first day, I had to worry about getting through the whole year.

CHAPTER FIVE

Movement

Delaney

By fifth period, I'd stopped being able to sit still. My new English/language arts teacher, Mr. Cervantes, read us the first chapter in *Alice's Adventures in Wonderland*, which I loved because it had lots of silly rhymes and even a talking rabbit in it. It made me daydream about having chats with Mynah. After all, she's named after a bird who talks. When he was done, he said there wasn't enough time to read the next chapter and we should just sit tight until the bell rang.

"Sit tight" always makes me imagine that I'm wearing a seat belt.

I tried to pretend that I was strapped into my chair, but my imagination failed me. The problem was that the sitting was going on too long. I'd already done it for five straight classes. Our twenty-five-minute lunch break barely gave me enough time to find my sisters, go through the food line, and eat my chicken enchilada before the next bell. No time to really move around and get out trapped wiggles.

I felt all wound up — almost literally. Like one of those toys where you wind the knob all the way to make it run or flip or shoot sparks out of its mouth, and even if you knock it on its side, it still has to move in some way.

Luckily I have some experience with the jitters and have developed methods of coping. These are the best ones:

Tapping Feet. This can really help let out the pent-up jitters, but people shouldn't do this if they have on noisy shoes. I was wearing my sneakers today, so that helped.

Wiggling Toes. This is what I do when I have on noisy shoes. Basically I just move my toes around. Sometimes I get carried away, though, and it turns into Tapping Feet.

Drumming Fingers. This is pretty classic, and I occasionally see other students doing it. I like tapping my fingertips on the desktop, trying out different rhythms and making sure it's not so loud that you bother people. A variation of this is to use pencils as drumsticks.

Bouncing Behind. Last year this worked great because we had Mrs. Svrcek for sixth period, and she always played music in her room. So when I'd bounce and wiggle in my chair, it looked like I was dancing. Only Mr. Cervantes wasn't playing music, and he already gave me a funny look when I went the long way around the room to get to the pencil sharpener. I didn't want him to think I was a troublemaker.

There's also Pretending You're Thirsty and Asking to Go to the Water Fountain, which is great because, like Pencil Sharpening, it lets you get up out of your chair and walk. Unfortunately, I'd already done that ten minutes ago. Also unfortunately, the water fountain was right across the hall from our classroom, so it didn't let me move that much. It works much better when it's way down at the end of the corridor.

Thinking about that gave me an idea. "Mr. Cervantes?" I said, raising my hand.

"Yes?"

"Is there anything you need done? Would you like me to hand out papers or collect papers or wipe down the black-boards? Or maybe I could run a secret message from you to the office? You could put it in a sealed envelope if you're afraid I'd look — which I wouldn't."

He smiled at me. "That's very nice of you, but there's nothing I need right now. Also, there's only a few minutes until the bell rings, so you probably wouldn't have time. Just sit back and relax."

I wanted to explain that I was super fast and could do lots of things in a few minutes *except* sit back and relax. But I didn't want him to think I was a problem. So I said, "Okay, but I hope you do think of me should you ever need someone for a special task or mission. I can provide references, if you need them."

For some reason, this made him laugh. While he was laughing, Tucker Burnett, who sat a couple of seats over, mumbled, "Teacher's pet." I gave him warning eyes, and he looked a little shamefaced. He's scared of Dawn, so maybe he was afraid I'd sic her on him.

It took doing Wiggling Toes, Tapping Feet, and Drumming Fingers all at the same time, but I managed to stay in my seat for the next few minutes. When the bell finally rang, I rocketed out of my chair, flew out the door, and raced down the hall.

I've gotten very good at a speedy walk that allows me to move fast but doesn't get me in trouble for running inside. The trick is to barely lift your knees and think of your feet as wheels.

I made it to the gym so fast, the only other person there was Coach Manbeck, the Cheer Squad teacher. She led the middle school transition camp, so I knew who she was. I liked how she was always smiling. She's really muscular, too, which makes her look like a superhero. At transition camp she told us she used to be a gymnast.

"Hi and welcome!" she said to me. "Are you new to Cheer Squad?"

"Yep! Well . . . actually I was signing up for a corn dog, but it worked out that I got the class."

She gave a confused smile. "Well, I'm sure glad you ended up here."

Just then I spotted Dawn. She took a step inside the gym and heaved a big sigh. When Coach Manbeck welcomed her, she said, "So I think you ought to know that I'm basically here against my will."

"Oh," Coach Manbeck said, her grin faltering even more. "Okay."

"I already told her about the corn dogs," I whispered to Dawn.

After that, a wave of students came in, one of them Darby. I was glad to be back with my sisters — especially since at lunch we only had time to eat, and no time to talk. But I was also sad knowing that we were missing Color Guard. Looking out the rectangular window, I could see them outside on the grass, lining up with their flags.

"All right, everyone," Coach Manbeck called out. "We'll be starting in a few minutes. In the meantime, feel free to stretch or run around."

"Run around?" At this I perked up. "Can we do cartwheels, too?" I asked.

"Of course," Coach Manbeck replied with a laugh. "In fact, I encourage it. You are all free to run and jump and stretch until I start the class."

I was so happy to hear this, I immediately sped away

and started turning cartwheels down the length of the gym. I found out later that Dawn wanted to use those few moments to talk strategy, only I took off before she could convene us.

It felt great to get all the pent-up jitters out of me. Not only did my muscles feel looser and warmer, but my brain felt more awake. I make good grades, but sometimes I think I'd be a genius if they'd let us do jumping jacks in class — or at least jog in the halls.

By the time I'd finished my second round of cartwheels, Coach Manbeck called us all to the bleachers. I sat between Dawn and Darby on the first row.

"Good afternoon, Cheer Squad!" Coach Manbeck shouted, and everyone clapped and whistled at that. I wondered if we were supposed to say everything like a cheer.

"Our first home game is in a month, so we have lots of practicing to do." Coach Manbeck handed out a sheet of paper with the football schedule on it.

I raised my hand and waved it around until Coach called on me. Then I asked her why some games were listed in heavy, bold type and others were in lighter type.

"That's a great question!" she cheered. "The bolded games are home games that will be played on our own school field. The others will be at other campuses — some of them pretty far away."

Then I asked her other questions, like how would the Cheer Squad get to the faraway schools, what does Cheer Squad do if it rains or snows, and why is it Cheer *Squad*, not

Cheer *Platoon* or *Posse*? She said the squad cheers only at home games, that the games are usually called off if the weather is bad, but sometimes we might have to cheer in light rain. Also, she didn't know why it was called a squad. It was just tradition. Each time I asked something she'd say, "Good question!" and smile. Her smile did dwindle a little every time I spoke until it went away.

Dawn elbowed me. "Why are you interrogating the poor woman?" she whispered. "We're not going to be in the class for very long, so none of this matters."

"I'm just a very curious person," I whispered back.

Coach Manbeck went on to explain other things. Apparently Cheer Squad is divided into two different groups. There are the eight cheerleaders, who stand on the sidelines and lead the crowd in chants and cheers. They're the ones who get to run and jump and stack on top of one another. The other group is called the Poms. They sit in a special section in the stands and cheer — plus, they get to wave around little pom-poms. Tryout for leaders would be held in three weeks. Anyone who didn't make it would get to be a Pom. Right now, until leaders were selected, all the new students were considered Poms.

Next, she had two girls model the official Cheer Squad uniforms. Poms wore navy-and-silver T-shirts with jeans and waved around glittery pom-poms, which made a big *shush* sound when you shook them. The leader uniform was a short-sleeved sweater on top and what looked like a skirt on the bottom — only it was really shorts with a skirt over it. I thought those were the coolest inventions ever. I don't wear skirts or dresses a lot, but now whenever I need to, I want to wear those kinds of skirts. That way I could do cartwheels and handstands anytime and not have to worry about being "indecent," as Mom calls it.

Suddenly Dawn raised her hand. "Can boys be in Cheer Squad?" she asked. When I gave her a surprised look, she whispered, "What? I'm curious about stuff, too."

"Great question!" Coach Manbeck said. "We love it when male students sign up for Cheer Squad. Unfortunately, none of them did this year."

"Maybe you could try luring them with pizza?" I suggested, but I'm not sure Coach heard me, since she didn't say anything to that.

"Any other questions?" Coach asked.

I raised my hand. "How come Cheer Squad only cheers for football and basketball?"

"Yeah," Dawn said. "Why not other sports?"

This time Coach didn't say *good question*. She just smiled and shrugged her shoulders. "That's how it's always been. It's tradition."

"That doesn't seem very fair," Dawn said.

Again, Coach Manbeck didn't seem to hear her. She went on to talk about their fundraising in the spring, but I missed a lot of what she said because Dawn was grumbling.

"The sooner we get out of this class, the better. I for one don't care to leap around clapping and hollering for something as silly as a football game. At least Color Guard is patriotic."

"*Shhh!*" Darby said. "Don't get us in trouble."

"Yeah, *shhh*," I said. "Besides, this is tradition — just like Color Guard."

Dawn crossed her arms over her chest. "Please. If you think . . ." Suddenly she stopped talking. Her eyes went wide and her mouth made an O shape. "Hello," she said, her voice going soft and sweet.

At first I was confused, but then I followed her gaze to where Coach Manbeck stood demonstrating the equipment. In her arms was a huge white megaphone.

CHAPTER SIX

Anti-Trust

Dawn

Hoo-boy," Mom said when she saw me carry the megaphone into the house. She was sitting on the floor of the living room with her back against the striped chair. On the coffee table in front of her sat her open laptop. "I really don't like the looks of that thing."

"It's for homework," I said.

"It is?" Delaney said. "Then how come I didn't get one? Or Darby?"

I shrugged. "You guys didn't ask."

I set the megaphone on the dining room table and ran my hand over the sleek white finish. It was a thing of beauty. It was kind of heavy and unwieldy, and it kept bonking people accidentally as I moved through the halls on our way out of school, but I didn't care. It was the best thing about that silly Cheer Squad — maybe even the best thing about seventh grade so far. I knew I could do great things with that big white cone, I just wasn't sure what they were yet.

Lily pushed through the door to the kitchen. Right behind her was Alex, her fiancé.

We all ran to him and hugged him, and Delaney bounced about, saying, "Alex! Alex! Alex!" the way she usually does when she sees him. He'd been working in Austin for a few weeks, and hadn't visited in a while.

"Hey there!" he greeted us, laughing.

"You're here!" Darby said.

"I am. I have a couple of days off and thought I'd go see my favorite people in the world not related to me."

"Not *yet* related," I corrected him.

I loved seeing Lily and Alex side by side. It's like they match — not like Darby, Delaney, and I match, though. Let's say they were in a big group of folks, all jumbled up together, and you had to pair up all the people for some reason. You'd put Lily and Alex together, even if you didn't know they were in love. Lily and Alex both have a sparkle to them. A special something that makes people feel good whenever they get near the two of them.

"So," Lily said, clapping her hands together, "tell us all about your first day of school." She and Alex sat on the couch and Lily patted the empty cushion on the other side of her.

"It was great!" Delaney said, leaping into the spot beside Lily.

"It was okay," Darby said, balancing on the armrest next to Delaney.

"It's hard to sum up in a few words," I said, flopping onto the chair behind Mom.

Lily laughed. "Fair enough. So how did you like Cheer Squad?"

"It was great!" Delaney said.

"I liked the jumping and cartwheeling," Darby said, "but I didn't like all the yelling."

"Are you kidding? The hollering was the best part," I said. "I thought all that jumping around was ludicrous."

"Still no schedule change?" Mom asked.

"We're trying," I said with a grumble. "But I don't think Mr. Plunkett feels it's a priority. I keep stopping by his office, but he just shakes his head and says, 'Not yet.'"

"Well, I hope you give Cheer Squad a fair chance," Lily said.

"You sound like Mr. Plunkett," I grouched.

"I mean it," she said. "We'd love to see you all cheering on the sidelines, wouldn't we?" She turned to Alex.

"That's right," he said. "We'd go cheer for the cheerleaders."

I noticed the smiles they had on their faces — the relaxed-happy looks they always got when they were around each other. It made my angry feelings go quiet. And it made me want to focus on something else — the kind of something that was nothing but good.

"So enough about us," I said. "When are you two getting married?"

Delaney immediately started bouncing on her end of the sofa. "Yeah, when? We want to help!"

"We can help pick out food," Darby suggested.

"Or help you decide on a dress," I added.

"Oh! I know!" Delaney raised her hand as if we were still in school. "We can even dress up and be flower girls again, only with real flowers this time."

"You girls are sweet." Lily smiled down at her hands and fiddled with her engagement ring. We waited to see if she would say anything more, but she didn't. Alex just kept looking at Lily. He was smiling, but it seemed kind of nervous.

"Oh! I know!" Delaney exclaimed, raising her hand again. "Tommy Ybarra said his aunt is getting married soon, and they're going to use lassos! So since Lucas has been giving us lasso lessons, and Darby's really good at it, maybe she could do that at the wedding."

"Yeah, I can help lasso you!" Now Darby was bouncing on the couch, too.

Mom, Lily, and Alex started laughing. "I think I know what Tommy is referring to. It's not the same kind of lassos as you're thinking about," Mom said. "There's no actual roping involved. The priest just lays the cords on the bride and groom. It's a lovely tradition."

"Oh." Delaney looked disappointed.

"Tradition," I mumbled. I thought I'd done it silently, but Mom must have heard me.

"Something wrong, Dawn?" she asked, turning around to look at me.

I sank down lower on the chair. My happiness at seeing Lily and Alex was starting to lose power. Once again I felt weighed down by all the frustration I'd been carrying around. Plus, I was still a little sore at Mom for not helping us out. "It's just . . . For some reason we keep hearing that word. *Tradition*. It makes me wonder, who gets to decide what becomes a tradition?"

Mom shrugged. "No one in particular. But I guess in a way we all do."

"Well, in that case, I think there should be a tradition that little sisters always get to help older sisters plan their weddings," I said with a nod.

"So can we help you guys?" Delaney asked Lily.

"Please?" Darby added, leaning past Delaney.

Lily suddenly jumped to her feet. "Oh, goodness! Alex, it's time for us to go."

"Oh. Right," Alex said, rising from the couch. "We should get moving."

Lily shouldered her woven bag and together they trotted toward the front door. "Sorry," Lily said as she stepped out onto the porch, "but we've got plans to meet some friends. Bye!" From behind her, we heard Alex say bye. Then the door shut. Soon we could hear Alex's car start up and drive away.

"Jiminy," I exclaimed, "Lily was moving like Delaney there."

Delaney flopped over onto the cushions Lily and Alex had just been sitting on. "I don't understand. Why won't she let us help her plan her wedding?"

"I think the answer is pretty clear," Darby said in a small, solemn voice. "She doesn't trust us after all the pandemonium we caused at her last wedding."

Delaney gasped. "Really?"

Mom set her computer on the coffee table and stood up to stretch. We all looked at her. It suddenly hit me how quiet she was on the matter.

"Mom, Lily wouldn't leave us out of the planning just because of a little mayhem from long ago, would she?" I asked.

"Well . . ." Mom's face crimped up as if she were wincing in pain. "I'm sure that doesn't help."

"But, but . . . we love Alex!" Delaney said. "We can't wait to see them get married! We wouldn't do anything to hurt their ceremony. Plus, we only caused that ruckus so that she and Alex would get back together!"

"Girls." Mom held up her hands like stop signs. "I know you want to help, but you need to let Lily do this her own way. After all, it's her wedding."

"But we should get to do *something*," I said. Darby and Delaney nodded.

Mom let out a long sigh. "Look, even if you don't get to

help, there's no reason to be upset. You love Lily and you love Alex and the important thing is that they're together — right?"

"I guess," Darby said.

"Sure," Delaney mumbled.

I hunched over, resting my chin on my hands, and made a vague noise that could be interpreted as an agreement.

But it wasn't.

"I call this meeting to order," I said, pounding my fist on my headboard.

"We sure are having a lot of these lately," Delaney said to Darby.

I ignored her and kept going. "This evening we convene to discuss a historic event: the wedding of our sister, the amazing Lily Brewster. First up on the agenda: How do we get to help plan the wedding? Anyone have ideas?"

Darby shook her head.

Delaney shook her head.

For a full minute, the three of us looked at one another. It was the sorriest meeting ever.

"Come on, gang," I said. "We have to be part of this — we just have to. And if they won't involve us, we'll have to figure out some way to help on our own. We've been part of a wedding before, so we know about the tasks involved."

"There's invitations, fancy outfits, cake . . ." Delaney counted on her fingers.

"But it wouldn't be right to just start ordering things for Lily and Alex," Darby said. "It's their wedding."

"Also, we have no money," Delaney added. "Also, we don't know when it will be yet. Or where. Basically, if you do the math, what we have equals zero info."

"There's got to be something we overlooked. Some important part we can play and start working on now." I frowned at the distant trees, where the sun was hiding behind. "I can try to wheedle more information out of Mom. Delaney, maybe you should ask Tommy and the other Ybarras about his aunt's wedding. And find out more about those lassos."

"Aye-aye."

"And Darby, you should do some research on the internet."

"Okay."

I studied Darby's thoughtful face as she made note of this on the pad of paper she was holding. "Actually, Darby, maybe you should go ask the Ybarras and Delaney can surf the internet."

Darby shrank back against the wall. "No, not me. Delaney's better at that stuff."

"She's right, you know," Delaney said to me. "And she's better at researching things online."

"But we're trying to get Darby to stop being such a fraidy cat around people. We all agreed."

"She's also right," Delaney said to Darby.

Darby looked down, hunching her shoulders. She

reminded me of a turtle trying to tuck its head into its shell. "But can't I do something else?" she mumbled. "Lily's wedding is just too important. You don't want me to accidentally make mistakes."

"She's right, too," Delaney said.

Darby did have a point. I tapped my finger against my chin, wondering what to do. Then finally, I got one of my brilliant ideas.

"Fine. Darby researches online and Delaney goes around asking folks. But" — here I paused for dramatic effect — "this means Darby has to go introduce herself to our new neighbors."

Darby gulped. "I do?"

"Yep. Right now."

CHAPTER SEVEN

House Representative

Darby

I used to think the brown-brick house down the road from us was really pretty, but as I trudged toward it late that afternoon, it seemed kind of menacing. The side facing the street had two high windows with awnings at the second-story level and a double front door below. It reminded me of a sinister creature with two heavily lidded eyes and a mouth wide enough to swallow me up.

I usually walk the slowest of my sisters, mainly because I like to look at things as we go. I find cool stuff this way, like interesting rocks or wildflowers or even money. Today, though, I was walking *extra* slow. I was nervous about knocking on the big mouthy door and talking to someone I'd never met. I can easily do things like that with my sisters beside me, mainly because they do most of the talking. But alone? The thought made a fuzzy feeling sweep over my face, and my hands trembled, rattling the shiny silvery gift bag I was holding.

We knew that when you first meet neighbors, you're supposed to bring something to give them, usually baked goods. We're not sure why, but it seems it's tradition. Delaney said it's a celebratory "welcome to the neighborhood" gift. I thought it was more of a "you're probably super busy moving in and can't find your pots and pans yet, so here's some food" gift. Dawn said it should be a "we're nice people, so please don't call the cops if you hear Delaney scream" gift.

Anyway, since we didn't have baked goods on hand, we put a box of chocolate Pop-Tarts in the bag. We figured it still counted because it was baked pastries, even if we didn't bake them.

Finally I ran out of road to walk down and was facing the house. As I gazed up at it, I felt what I first thought was an earthquake, but it was just my limbs going jittery. I thought about running into the trees next to the yard and living with the raccoons for as long as I wanted to . . . or at least until the Pop-Tarts ran out.

Suddenly I heard from behind me, "Keep moving!" It was Dawn's unmistakable voice, over the megaphone. They were watching me from the edge of our yard.

I knew they were right. I had to get over my shyness. Someday I was going to be chief justice of the U.S. Supreme Court, and to do that, I had to be able to look strangers in the eye and talk to them. But then, justices wear long robes, so no one would see if my knees were shaking. Today I was wearing shorts.

I stepped off the curb and headed down the sidewalk toward the front door. At the top of the driveway was a bicycle. It was a pretty aqua color and had a metal basket hanging from the handlebars. It was so lovely, it made me feel better. Anyone who had a bicycle like that couldn't be too bad. But even though I felt a little braver, I still held the gift bag in front of me with both hands, like a shield, as I approached.

The big front door was set in a nook. I felt like I was getting swallowed up, even though the recessed porch was all decorated with potted plants and a welcome mat that actually said WELCOME. There was also a ceramic garden gnome with a white beard and tall red hat, whose right hand gestured toward the door. Actually, the garden gnome was a little creepy. His eyes seemed to follow me, and I couldn't tell if he was smiling in a happy way or a sinister way.

"Here goes," I said to myself. Or maybe I said it to the gnome.

The double doors were right in front of me, but for some reason I couldn't knock. On either side were rectangles of glass — only not glass you can see through, more like the bubbly looking glass they make shower doors out of. I wondered if someone inside could see my shadow. Maybe they'd just open the door on their own? If they did, what would I say? I could say hi . . . and then what? My brain couldn't think of anything. And that was a major problem. I couldn't just say hi, shove some Pop-Tarts into the person's hands, and then walk away.

My breath was all fast and ragged and my feet started stepping backward all on their own. A thought came into my mind. *My sisters can't see me.* It was true! I could say I knocked, but the people weren't home. Only . . . Dawn would probably make me come back. So maybe I should say that they were home and were nice. I could say I gave them our baked treats and they thanked me.

But what would I do with the gift bag? I couldn't bring it back or they'd know I fibbed.

I turned all different directions, trying to decide. Finally I just left it hanging on the gnome's outstretched arm and ran out of there.

When I got to the road, I started walking again. My shaky nervousness about meeting people had gone away, but now I felt a new shaky nervousness about lying to my sisters. Plus, since I'm terrible at lying, I knew they'd see the truth the second they laid eyes on me.

My feet started slowing down again. I was not looking forward to seeing Dawn and Delaney. As I came around the bend, I was relieved to see they weren't in the yard anymore. Mom probably heard the megaphone and made them come inside. That bought me some time.

"Good evening!"

I was so lost in thought that the voice made me jump, even though it was friendly. Glancing in the direction it came from, I saw our neighbor, Mrs. Neighbor, sitting on one of the white wicker chairs she keeps on her porch.

Mr. and Mrs. Neighbor have lived across the street from us our whole lives. Before they retired, they were teachers. Mrs. Neighbor taught reading and Mr. Neighbor taught math. Whenever Mr. Neighbor sees me and my sisters walking into town together, going single file so that we won't stick out in the road and get hit by cars, he calls out, "Make way for ducklings!" And they always let us play in their sprinklers when it's hot out and offer us lemonade or ice cream during the breaks. For some reason, though, we didn't spend as much time doing that this past summer. Probably because we were hanging out with Lucas more, or helping Aunt Jane with her move.

Realizing that made me feel kind of bad, and my feet made the decision to walk over to Mrs. Neighbor instead of continuing toward home. I trotted down her walkway and stood at the base of her porch steps. "Hi, Mrs. Neighbor," I said. "How are you?"

"Fine, fine. How was the first day of school?" she asked.

I lifted one of my shoulders. "Okay, I guess. Not as good as other first days of school."

"Aw, I'm sorry to hear that," she said. She gestured toward the other chairs on her porch. "Why don't you come up and chat for a while? I could pour you a glass of iced tea and . . ."

That's all I heard. Because right at that moment, a movement caught my eye. I turned my head and saw someone coming down the road on a bicycle — an aqua-colored bicycle. And inside the front metal basket sat a shiny, silvery gift bag.

I panicked. It's the only explanation I have for what happened next.

As soon as I recognized the bike and our gift, I knew it was the new neighbor, and I didn't want that person to see me. So, quick as a flash, I dove behind the hedges that surrounded Mrs. Neighbor's front porch.

I stayed crouching in the dirt, with leaves and twigs poking me everywhere. As the bicycle came closer, I could see the person riding it. She had a familiar haircut — short in the back and long in the front. Wanda, the girl from my history class!

Once her bicycle was way down the road, I slowly crawled back out onto the sidewalk.

"Darby, honey?" Mrs. Neighbor was staring at me with wide, worried eyes. "Are you okay?"

I realized how crazy I probably looked, so I figured I owed her an explanation. "Well . . . I am, but at the same time I'm not," I said. I climbed the porch steps and sat down in one of the other wicker chairs. As I sipped a glass of iced tea that she offered, I told her about how my sisters were trying to help me get over my shyness, and how they told me to go introduce myself to the new neighbors — only I couldn't go through with it, and it made me feel ashamed. So when I saw Wanda, I decided to hide.

"I see." Mrs. Neighbor nodded. She didn't seem so alarmed anymore, just thoughtful. "You know, I think it's nice your sisters are trying to help you."

"I kind of wish they wouldn't," I said. "I can't help being like this. I'm just shy. I know I'm going to have to get over it at some point, but why do I have to change right now?"

Mrs. Neighbor shrugged. "I suppose you don't have to. But let me ask you this: If you're not able to approach people you don't know, won't you get lonely?"

"No," I said. "I have my sisters."

"That's true. But what about that person on the bicycle? What if she *doesn't* have sisters and would really like to meet someone?"

I had no answer to that. I'd never really considered it before.

What if Wanda was lonely?

CHAPTER EIGHT

Right to Assemble

Delaney

The next day was the back-to-school pep rally, so we each had to wear our blue Pom Squad shirts along with nice jeans and sneakers.

"These pants are uncomfortable," Dawn said as she walked in a somewhat bowlegged fashion toward the bus stop. "And short."

We had grown a bit since Mom bought the jeans last spring, and they felt a little tight — even tighter after breakfast, when I ate two bowls of Frosted Mini-Wheats. Plus, while they used to come down to our feet, they now ended just above the ankles.

"It's okay. No one will notice," I said. "Only shy people like Darby walk around looking down. And shy people are too shy to make fun of someone because of their pants — even if they think it in their heads."

Darby agreed with my theory. "Even though I'm trying not to be shy anymore, I'd still never make fun of someone's pants."

Dawn and I patted her back. We knew she still felt bad about not being able to go through with meeting the new neighbors. As disappointed as we were that she backed out — and that she wasted a perfectly good box of Pop-Tarts — we were proud of her for being honest with us. That couldn't have been easy.

As the bus pulled up to school, we noticed that a lot of the other students were wearing school colors. The eighth-grade cheerleaders were in uniform and the Color Guard also had on their navy blue outfits. Dawn made a grumbling sound whenever one of them walked by. I suggested we keep a lookout for any Color Guard members who looked like they weren't having fun, thinking we might be able to convince them to quit. Unfortunately, they all looked happy or excited.

We followed a few more Cheer Squad members into the gym. Everyone who was part of the pep rally was supposed to report there early. Four kids from band showed up with drums strapped to them, and as we practiced cheers and chants, they pounded out rhythms. I had to admit, it sounded pretty cool.

Coach Manbeck blew her whistle and told the Pom Squad to get into position for the rally. Only those who were cheerleaders last year got to be on the floor of the gym. The rest of us were given the small glittery pom-poms and sat in a big square section on the bleachers. I sat in the front row, next to Dawn. Darby sat on her other side.

After that, the Color Guard got into formation and their teacher made them run through some moves real quick as the drum corps played. It hurt to watch, knowing we were supposed to be with them.

"Look at those guys," Dawn said, shaking her head. "Sloppy, sloppy."

I thought they looked good, and was about to say so, but then I realized Dawn just had sour grapes because we didn't get into the class.

Darby put her arm around Dawn. "I know. I wish I was twirling with them, too. But don't worry. We'll get in there eventually."

"Yeah," I said, putting my arm around her from the other direction. "Besides, cheerleading is tradition, too. Think about that."

"It's not the same. Color Guard has honor. Cheer Squad just gets people fired up about football and basketball, which, if you ask me, people are already too fired up about in these parts. If only they . . ." She stopped all of a sudden, her mouth hanging open, eyes wide. "Wait," she said. "I think I'm being brilliant again."

I was about to ask her what she meant when there was a

loud crackling sound overhead. Mrs. Jessup's voice came over the intercom, telling all the students to report to the pep rally in the gym before they went to class. Immediately students began streaming through the double doors, laughing and talking and climbing all over the bleachers, so it was too loud to hear any particular voice.

When most everyone was sitting down, the drummers started drumming and the cheerleaders started a loud cheer. This was our cue to wave the pom-poms to the beat. As we did this, the football team came in and sat on the folding chairs. They were all wearing nice shirts; some even had on ties. I guess it was like their dress uniform.

Mr. Carrothers, the football coach, walked up to a microphone on a stand and said, "Presenting your proud Patriots! This year they will represent this school and WIN! Give them a big hand!"

At that the whole crowd started hooting and applauding, and the cheerleaders started leading the "Let's Get Fired Up!" chant.

The noise was wonderful. The vibrations from the drums, claps, and stamps shook through my body, and energy was building up inside me — a big, fizzy, electric feeling. As it kept building, I kept bouncing higher and higher in my seat. But that wasn't enough movement to let the energy out. I was starting to worry that I might explode in a meteor shower of glitter pom-poms and Frosted Mini-Wheats.

"Let's get fired up!" Clap, clap! Stomp, stomp!

Digga-digga, digga-digga, whomp! Whomp! Whomp!

I bounced and chanted and waved my pom-poms so enthusiastically, Dawn kept having to duck. Staying in place was getting harder and harder to do.

Finally I couldn't take it anymore. I had to do something. Before I could argue with myself, I was on my feet jumping and shouting and turning cartwheels. Only . . . I forgot that I was wearing my too-small jeans instead of shorts. When I stood up after my roundoff, everything felt kind of breezy below my waist and something was flapping against my legs. I glanced down and saw that my pants had ripped open at the leg seam. Luckily the split hadn't yet reached as high as my yellow underpants with the orange happy rabbit faces. But the rip seemed to be getting longer and longer . . .

Thankfully, Darby and Dawn noticed what was happening. They jumped to their feet and stood in front of me, jumping up and down as if they were super excited, too.

"Go out the side door," Darby hollered back to me. "Run to the dressing room!"

Her face was all pink, and I realized she must love me very much to be jumping around and drawing attention away from me and over to herself. Quick as I could, I ran out the side door to the locker room. The metal door slammed behind me with a *blam*!

I sat on a bench and examined the long tears in my jeans. The sounds were almost gone, and so was the sparkly, bubbly excitement I'd felt. As glad as I was that nobody saw my underwear, I was also feeling sad about missing the rest of the pep rally. It was the most fun I'd had in a long time.

CHAPTER NINE

Policy Shift

Dawn

Why do they call them burritos?" Delaney asked as she considered her lunch. We sat at the end of one of the cafeteria tables, Darby and I on one side and Delaney across from us.

"I'm not sure," Darby said between bites. "The word means 'little donkey' in Spanish."

Delaney gasped. "I'd never eat a donkey. Big or little."

Over spring break we'd gone camping at Lake Lewis, where Aunt Jane was living now. While we were there, Delaney made friends with a donkey we called Mo. She still talks about him all the time, and when we write Aunt Jane, she includes a letter to Mo and asks Aunt Jane to read it to him.

"Enough about burritos. I'm calling this meeting to order," I said, pounding my fist twice on the tabletop, making the Jell-O on our lunch trays jiggle.

"Why are we having another meeting?" Delaney asked, with her mouth full.

I gave her a stern stare.

"What I mean is" — Delaney swallowed — "why are we having a meeting now?"

"I have important business to discuss," I said.

"Do I have to take notes?" Darby asked. "Because I'm hungry."

"No," I replied.

"Is this about my blunder at the pep rally?" Delaney asked. I noticed her absently hike up the waist of the sweat pants Coach Manbeck had lent her. "Because by the way, thank you. You guys saved my rear. I owe you big-time."

"That's also not the reason for the meeting," I said. "But what the blazes happened to you out there anyway?"

"Yeah," Darby said. "What made you do that?"

Delaney shrugged. "I don't really know. It's like I exploded with excitement. You know how I have to run and jump around if I'm upset or nervous? It was like that — only with good feelings."

"I suppose that's all fine and dandy," I said. "But in the future, make sure you're wearing stretchier pants."

"I will."

From behind Delaney, I could see two girls coming toward us, Cherry Luedecke and Lynette Barstow. They were two of the eighth-grade cheerleaders who helped us learn the chants in sixth period. As they approached, they were looking right at Delaney, and I wondered if they were going to give her a hard time about the pep rally.

"Hi!" Cherry said, grinning down at Delaney. "Were you the one who did that great run on the gym floor this morning?"

Delaney hunched her shoulders in a Darby sort of way. I could tell she was also worried they'd scold her or make fun of her. "Um . . . maybe?"

"That was awesome!" Cherry said.

"Yeah. I hope you go out for cheerleader," Lynette said. "You'd be perfect."

Delaney's mouth hung open slightly and her eyes focused on a spot of nothingness in the distance. It's not often Delaney is speechless, so I could tell she was really uncomfortable. It was time to rescue her again.

I leaned across the table and waved my hand to get Cherry's and Lynette's attention. "Thank you for your interest, but I'm afraid Delaney has other plans," I said. "The thing is, we're not going to be in Cheer Squad for very long."

The girls' smiles fell away. "Really?" Lynette said, looking surprised. "That's too bad."

"Yeah. Well . . . nice run anyway," Cherry said. "See you."

"Bye. See you in class," Delaney said.

I also said good-bye and Darby added a shy wave as they turned and walked back the way they came.

"You didn't have to tell them that," Delaney said to me.

"No problem. I was glad to get you out of that situation. Now finally we can have our meeting." I pounded my fist on the table two more times. "I hereby call us to order once again."

As soon as I said that, another girl walked past us, behind Delaney. She had an interesting hairstyle — long in front and short in back. She waved as she went by, and Darby waved back.

Delaney turned to look, but by that time, the girl had disappeared into the throng by the salad bar.

"You know what?" Darby said. "Maybe we should invite other people to sit with us."

I frowned. "Why would we do that?"

"Just . . . because," Darby said, lifting her right shoulder in a lopsided shrug. "It would be nice."

"But we're trying to have a private meeting!" I didn't intend to sound grouchy, but I was tired of all the interruptions. "How can you have a private meeting if you invite just anyone to listen in?"

"Fine," Darby said, hunkering over her lunch tray. "So what's this big idea you have, Dawn?"

I cleared my throat and sat up straight. After glancing right and left to make sure no one else was listening, I said, "Prepare yourself to hear one of the most genius ideas I've gotten in a long while. It came to me during the pep rally. I'm thinking, if we're going to be part of Cheer Squad, even for a little while, we should instigate some changes — for the better."

"Like what?" Delaney asked.

"You know how the Cheer Squad only shows up for football or basketball games?" I asked.

"Um, yeah?"

"Well, I think it's high time we fix that. In the interest of fairness, and to maximize school spirit, I say we start cheering for all the teams at school."

Delaney looked confused. "But Coach Manbeck said —"

"I know what she said. And we don't need her. We can get a group together, show up, and cheer on our own. It's just demonstrating school spirit, and there's nothing wrong with that, right?"

"I guess not," Darby said, only her voice went up high at the end of her sentence, as if she were asking a question.

"Oh, I see. We'll be bonus spirit boosters! Brewster boosters! Brewsters who boost!" Delaney danced around in her seat. "When do we start?"

I tapped my chin. "I haven't figured that out yet. But it shouldn't be hard. We just need to find some poor, underappreciated sport that we can cheer for. As long as we're stuck in Cheer Squad, we're going to make our time count. Agreed?"

"Agreed," Delaney said.

"Agreed," Darby said.

The bell rang right at that minute, and even though I'd only taken four bites of my burrito, I didn't mind. For the first time since school started, I felt a sense of mission and duty.

Maybe this was why our schedules had been botched up. Maybe we were meant to make a difference.

CHAPTER TEN

House Oversight

Darby

Our first weekend after school started was a Dad weekend — the first one in three weeks. So when school let out on Friday, we jumped into Dad's VW bus as he drove through the pickup circle and gave him quick hugs around the neck before strapping ourselves into our seats.

In addition to our school stuff, we each carried small overnight bags with a couple of changes of clothes that Mom made us pack, since most of Dad's belongings — including the things we kept there — were still in boxes.

For two years after Mom and Dad divorced, Dad lived in a two-bedroom apartment. But earlier this summer, he bought a house. It's single-story with dark red brick and was built in 1950. Dad calls it *ranch style*, but I don't know why, since it's near the center of town, and there aren't any horses or cattle nearby. When you walk in the front door, you step into a living room/dining room area with a kitchen in the back, separated by a low half wall. To the left is a long hall-way that leads to three small bedrooms and a bathroom with flamingo-pink tile. To the right is a converted garage that Dad is using as both his bedroom and an office, with a whole area full of shelves where he can store the medical supplies he sells. There's even a yard for Quincy — only it's not fenced in yet, so until it is, he can't come over.

"Did our new beds arrive?" was the first thing Dawn said to Dad after hello.

"Not yet," he said, pulling the bus onto the road. We bounced left and right in our seat.

"Dagnabbit." Dawn scowled out the window. "What's taking them so long?"

I knew she was looking forward to getting the bed she'd picked out of the catalog — the one with the super tall wooden headboard with a scroll pattern carved into it. She probably couldn't wait to bang her fist on it to call our meetings to order.

Delaney, meanwhile, picked out a four-poster bed so she could swing and twirl around the posts, and I'd selected a white metal canopy bed with curtains that could be pulled shut all around it. I loved the idea of my own private pillowy place.

"Actually, I'm relieved they haven't arrived yet, since we still have to paint your rooms," Dad said. "But we can prob-ably finish that this weekend."

That's another cool thing we each got to decide on — new colors for our bedroom walls. Delaney had quickly picked out a soft yellow shade, like lemonade. Dawn chose a cool blue called Lake that looked nothing like the inky lake water we were used to, but was still pretty. And I'd found a light, dreamy lilac that reminded me of twilight.

We were supposed to be doing the walls ourselves — with Dad's help, of course — cleaning and priming and measuring and buying paint. Unfortunately, Dad had to travel a lot toward the end of summer, so we didn't finish before school started, like we'd hoped to. This probably meant we'd be "camping" in the living room again for the next couple of nights, since paint fumes can dissolve your brain.

"Home sweet home!" Dad sang out as he pulled into his new driveway. I liked how happy and proud he seemed, and the way he kept referring to his house as his "quaint abode." He even didn't seem to mind too much that he had to sell his Vespa scooter in order to help raise the down payment. Although I kind of miss getting rides on it.

"Tonight I'm making my masterpiece hamburgers," Dad announced as he unlocked the door. I could see that he'd gotten a new lamp, but otherwise everything looked just like the last time we were there. In fact, playing cards were still spread across the coffee table from our game of Spite and Malice.

"Will you make potato wedges?" I asked.

"Already fried up," Dad said.

"And pickles?" Dawn asked.

"Two kinds in the refrigerator."

"And root beer?" Delaney asked.

Dad's grin went slack. "Ah . . . no. Sorry. Afraid I don't have any."

I felt bad, like we'd spoiled some of the fun.

"We could walk to the Corner Mart and buy some," Dawn suggested.

"Yes! Yes! Yes!" Delaney hopped in a small circle. "Please? Can we?"

"Sure, but be careful," Dad said, handing them a five-dollar bill.

"We will."

Dawn and Delaney opened the door and headed down the front stoop. "Come on, Darby," Delaney said, glancing back at me.

"I'm going to stay here and help," I said. We hadn't seen Dad in a while, and it seemed wrong to leave him when we'd only just got there.

"Suit yourself," Dawn said with a shrug and shut the door.

Dad was in the kitchen, whistling a rock 'n' roll song I kind of recognized. He was crouched in front of the open refrigerator, pulling burger patties, pickles, and sliced cheeses off the shelves and setting them on the counter.

"What can I do to help?" I asked.

"Hmm . . . I'm not sure," he said, straightening up and shutting the fridge. "I think everything is pretty much set. All I need to do is grill the meat. But you know what you could do? You could unpack a box or two in the living room. There's one with your fall clothes in it. Should be marked."

"Okeydokey," I said, saluting him. He saluted me back. Soon the whistling started up again and I could hear him chopping something.

I found our clothes in a box marked DDD DUDS. It was crammed full of jeans and tops and even some old costumes. As I pulled out each piece, one by one, some of them triggered a memory. There was the black T-shirt with a cat in an astronaut helmet, floating in space, that I'd worn to Lucas's tenth birthday party. There was the pair of Delaney's jeans that ripped in the knee when she tried to pet Old Mr. Maroney's rooster and ended up running for her life. At the bottom of the box were the bathrobes we got on a trip to Oolie's Water Kingdom two summers ago. They're made out of the same plushy white material as towels. On the front is the castle logo, and the words on the back read "No P in Our Poolies!" with *X*s over the letter *P*s. It made me smile to see them, and I remembered how much fun we'd had on that trip.

Suddenly I realized the clothes looked smaller than I remembered. As I held a pair of pants up against me, my smile wilted. The bottoms came up above the ankles. I tried pulling some tops over my head, but my head was too big. Some T-shirts were so old, they featured pictures from cartoons we didn't even watch anymore.

I walked back into the kitchen to tell Dad. To demonstrate how bad it was, I wore an Oolie's bathrobe. The sleeves came down to just past my elbow, and the belt tied around my chest instead of my belly.

He cracked up when he saw me. "I guess you girls will be needing some new clothes for over here. I probably should have thought of that. Need to borrow some of mine for the weekend?"

I smiled and rolled my eyes. "No, we brought enough with us."

Next we measured how tall I was next to him. I was finally up to his shoulders! We even compared feet, but his shoes were still way bigger than mine. Dad said he wasn't going to grill the burgers until Dawn and Delaney returned from the store, so we went back into the living room together to unload more boxes.

"Ah, here's a good one. Let's unpack this," he said, lifting a box onto the coffee table. MEMENTOS was written on all sides in black marker.

We stood side by side as he sliced through the packing tape with his pocketknife and opened the flaps. Looking into the box, I saw a face staring back at me. I laughed and lifted out a framed picture.

"Oh my. I'd forgotten about that one," Dad said, grinning and shaking his head.

It was a work of art that Dawn had done in second grade. I remember we were supposed to paint our heroes and do a presentation. Dawn, of course, did a portrait of George Washington. She worked really hard on it, wanting to get the white hair, broad face, and long nose just right. When it came time to present, she held it up proudly and said to our class,

"I'm sure you all know who this is." There was a long silence, and then a boy named Aiden said, "Your grandma?"

Dawn had gotten so frustrated, she insisted on going back to the craft table and painting the name at the bottom of the picture — only people probably shouldn't paint while mad, because she accidentally spelled it *George Washigton*. When she realized her mistake, she got even madder. In fact, she's still embarrassed about it. But Dad loved the picture and insisted on framing it.

Also in the box were some framed photos of us, three plaster handprints, some baby clothes, a poster tube of Delaney's long butcher paper drawing showing how a bill becomes a law, and a big tin containing all the finger puppets I made of the nine U.S. Supreme Court justices.

Even though Dad and I were both smiling and laughing, another feeling was coming over me, one I couldn't quite identify. My eyes went warm and wet, and my insides felt crumpled, as if all those memories were jabbing me in the stomach.

I stared down at the sculpture I'd just pulled from the box. I remembered I'd made it long ago, but I couldn't remember what it was. It looked like a big poodle with a squashed face. As I studied it, the image went blurry and my throat went tight.

Suddenly I couldn't do any more. I set the mushed-up dog-blob on the table and plopped down on the sofa.

"Darby, sweetie. You okay?" My vision was too clouded

with tears to see Dad's face clearly, but his voice sounded concerned.

"I'm fine," I said, wiping my eyes. "It's only . . ." I stopped, unsure what to say. It wasn't just seeing all the relics from my past that got me all misty-eyed; it was also Dad's having a new place, my clothes not fitting anymore, and no Vespa. Only I didn't know how to explain all that. It wasn't like I loved those old clothes better than all the clothes in the world. And I understood that he had to sell the Vespa to help pay for the house. Plus, it was a really nice house. My emotions were all out of whack.

"Dad? Why does remembering happy stuff also make me feel a little sad at the same time?"

"Ah." Dad sat down beside me and put a hand on my shoulder. "That's nostalgia."

"Nostalgia," I repeated. "I've heard of that. What does it mean?"

"It's a complicated emotion, where you feel joy and sadness together. See, even though the memories are happy, you're all wistful because they're over and you can't ever go back to that time."

More tears filled my eyes. That was it exactly. I loved all those moments, but I also sort of missed them. "Do you ever feel nostalgia?"

"Every day," he said, patting my back. "Time can be a real rascal."

I nodded. "Yeah, time is weird. Sometimes, like when I'm

at school waiting for the bell to ring, or waiting for Christmas, or waiting for Aunt Jane to show up for a visit, time is super slow. But other times it goes fast. Too fast."

"Tell me about it," he said. "The reason I never unpacked this box of mementos was because I thought I'd only be in that apartment for a few months. Next thing I knew, two years had gone by."

"Yeah."

We sat there, side by side, surrounded by keepsakes and not saying anything. After a while, I felt better. It's as if the sad feelings were leaves that dried up and dropped, and my happy feelings were the tree that was left standing — rough and spindly, but strong.

"Buffalo!" I shouted.

Dad looked confused.

I pointed to the sculpture I'd set on the coffee table. The memory had finally come to me. "It's a buffalo," I explained. "I made it in third grade. Her name is Buffy."

He picked up the sculpture and grinned at it. "Well, hello there, Buffy," he said. Then he got to his feet, strode across the room, and carefully set her on a bookshelf. "Welcome home."

CHAPTER ELEVEN

Intelligence Report

Delaney

On Monday at school, I'd already finished my homework in fifth period and was tapping out a nice rhythm with Dancing Feet when Mr. Cervantes asked, "Can I get a volunteer to run these papers to the office for me?" I leaped out of my seat and ran up to him before he'd said the *e* part of *me*.

After I ran the errand lickety-split, I decided to take the long way back to class, just to use up more time. On the way, I passed Dawn in her math class. I only had a view of the back of her head, though, so she didn't see me. Then I passed Darby in her science class. I could see her face, but she was staring out the nearby window, chin in hand. She was so busy daydreaming, she didn't notice me, even when I waved both my arms.

It was strange seeing my sisters when they didn't know I was there. I guess it was kind of like spying, but not in a mean way. I just missed them. Going through a school day without them beside me felt weird and wrong — like I'd forgotten to wear pants.

At least my sisters and I had Cheer Squad together. Remembering that made me feel a little better.

A big shape was loping toward me from the far end of the hallway. Thinking it was a teacher, I stopped watching Darby and started walking toward class again. Then the big shape waved at me and I realized it was Rowdy Buchanan — an eighth-grade boy. Rowdy has had his nickname so long, I forgot what his real name was. I did remember that I didn't like him very much, though. In elementary school, he was always pushing people. He seems to have stopped that, but he's still not very nice.

"Hey, Insaney," he said to me. His voice was nice, but Insaney was his mean nickname for me. I scowled back at him.

"Hey yourself," I grumbled.

"What are you doing out here?" he asked, still not noticing that I was mad at him.

"Doing a favor for my teacher. What are you doing?"

"I had to see Plunkett for a schedule change." He waved a yellow sheet of paper in his hand. "I'm tall enough for basketball now, so I'm getting out of Color Guard."

My face exploded a little. My eyes got big, my mouth opened wide, and my whole head jutted forward as far as it would go. It was just the news we were waiting to hear!

I thanked Rowdy for the information and headed to see Mr. Plunkett. More specifically I said, "*Aaaaah!* Ohmigosh!

Yay! Thanks, Rowdy, gotta go!" and boinged toward the counselor's office.

The door was open when I got there. I poked my head around the corner to take a peek, but Mr. Plunkett glanced up and saw me.

"Hi, Dawn. Need anything?"

I walked over to his desk. "I'm Delaney. And yes, I need you to put us into Color Guard, please. I just saw Rowdy and he said he was getting out."

"I see." Mr. Plunkett took off his glasses and started cleaning them with a tissue. "But I'm afraid there's a problem."

Suddenly I worried that I'd messed up. Usually Dawn talks to the adults as our official spokesperson. Darby's too shy and I talk fast and don't always think about my words. All through fifth grade, Dawn and Darby banned me from speaking to grown-ups on behalf of us triplets after I tried to high-five Ms. Mendoza, the school clerk, and ended up knocking her cell phone into the fish tank. I'm allowed to talk on our behalf now, but only if Dawn isn't available.

"Wait, I'm sorry. I meant to say please. Please could you put us in Color Guard?"

His mouth made a little bend, which I figured was a smile. "Actually that's not the problem," he said. "The problem is that there are three of you but only one opening."

"Ohhh, right. Sorry. I guess sometimes I think of me and my sisters as all one person."

"But you're not."

"I know we're not. I know it. I just sometimes forget and don't think. Especially when I get overexcited. Like this time." I was babbling, and I knew it. "The thing is, my sisters and I are all for one and one for all. But I know that one isn't the same as three. Math is my best subject. English is the one I have to work hardest at."

"I understand. Where are you supposed to be right now, Delaney?"

"Um . . . English."

"Perhaps you should go back to class. If you or another of your sisters would like to sign up for Color Guard, come back after school or sometime tomorrow. Okay?"

"Okay. But Mr. Plunkett?"

"Yes?"

"If you get two more openings, you'll let us know, right?"

"I promise."

"Then let's shake on it." I started to put out my hand and then stopped. "Actually . . . can we high-five on it?"

His mouth went bendy again. "Sure."

I glanced all around, making sure nothing breakable or spillable was in my path. Then I reached up and whacked his hand with mine.

It felt good. Because even though we still couldn't get into Color Guard, I at least managed to high-five him without causing any damage.

CHAPTER TWELVE

Recruiting

Dawn

Delaney told us about the open spot in Color Guard class as soon as she got to Cheer Squad. Well, actually, she first told us all about her Dancing Feet and did a little demonstration. Then she got distracted trying to remember Rowdy's real name. After some rambling, she eventually got to the part where she talked to Mr. Plunkett.

"Dang," I said. "I should have been there."

"It wouldn't have made a difference. There would still be just one opening in the class," Delaney said.

I wasn't so sure. I knew I could have done a better job talking with Mr. Plunkett. In fact, I'm still not convinced Darby and I should ever have lifted that ban on Delaney talking to adults.

"Why don't you take the open spot, Delaney?" Darby said. "It's only fair since you're the one who heard about it first."

I didn't think that sounded fair at all. I started to grouch about it, but then Delaney said, "No way. If anything, Dawn should take it. She's put in the most work toward getting us a schedule change." That sounded fair to me.

But when they both looked at me and waited for my response, I shook my head. "Nope. It's all for one and one for all," I said. "Either we all get into the class or none of us do. Besides, we're already separated enough as it is."

"That's the truth," Darby mumbled.

"And in the meantime, we're going to make the best of Cheer Squad and change it for the better," I added.

At that moment, Coach Manbeck blew her whistle and told us all to listen up. "Attention, class. Today, for added fun, we're going to break into small groups!" For some reason, she said everything as if it should be followed by applause. "Each of our eighth-grade cheerleaders will lead a group and teach you a new cheer. When I blow my whistle, grab a couple of friends nearby and go and find yourself a station. I want to see which group learns it the fastest!"

She blew her whistle again and there was a mad scramble.

"Delaney, come work with me!" Lynette Barstow came out of nowhere, grabbed Delaney's hand, and pulled her to another section of the gym.

"Can you believe the nerve?" I said to Darby after they'd run off. "Stealing our sister right out from under us."

Darby made an *oh, well* expression. "Lynette just wants to have the best group, and she knows Delaney is really good."

"And you're saying we aren't really good?" I asked. Darby's mouth started opening and closing, as if she were testing out words. "Never mind," I added. "Don't answer that."

Darby and I ended up with Cherry Luedecke's group. Only Cherry spent most of her time paying attention to Lynette and her group, who were standing nearby. After a while, Cherry and Lynette just sort of combined groups, with Cherry and Lynette leading and all the older students, plus Delaney, up front by them. Darby and I hung back with the other seventh graders, like Riley Cook and Aurelia Chavez.

"Will you two try out for cheerleader?" Aurelia asked.

"Probably not," I said.

"You'd rather stay in Pom Squad?" Riley asked.

I shook my head. "Nope. Hopefully we won't stay in that."

They looked a little confused and like they didn't know what else to say, so they turned their attention back toward Cherry. I didn't mind, since it spared me telling them the long, tragic story of how we ended up in Cheer Squad all because of Delaney's hankering for a corn dog.

While Cherry started showing us the arm movements for the "Attack That Quarterback" chant, I leaned toward Darby and whispered, "I'm going to stretch my legs and try to gather info for Operation Cheer-for-All."

She gave me a worried look.

"It'll just take a second," I reassured her.

I wandered over to a bulletin board on the wall by the double doors. It had all kinds of things pinned to it — lots of first aid tips and warnings about the importance of staying hydrated. There was also a copy of the lyrics to "Patriots Fight," which is our school song, a photo of last year's winning basketball team, and a calendar of sporting events for the month — which was exactly what I was hoping to find. Now all I had to do was find a sorry, overlooked team who could use some cheering.

"Hi, Dawn." Coach Manbeck's voice startled me. I hadn't heard her walk up. "Did you happen to bring that megaphone back?" she asked.

"Whoops. Sorry." I smiled sheepishly. "Did you need that?"

"Well . . . we had enough for today. But we will need it by the next pep rally, when we've chosen our additional cheerleaders."

"Okeydokey. No worries. You'll have it back by then."

As she turned to continue her rounds of the small groups, I stopped her. "Coach Manbeck? I was thinking, what if we added a few more events to the cheer schedule."

She frowned. "More events?"

"Yeah. To, you know, allow for more practice for new people like me." I tried to emphasize the benefit I thought she would appreciate most of all.

Coach Manbeck laughed. "I like your attitude. But I'm afraid our calendar is already full. At this point it wouldn't be fair for me to add more required events that take place outside the school day."

"What about bonus cheering?"

"Bonus cheering?"

"You know, cheering that isn't required but that happens out of a sense of duty. I mean, wouldn't you say that the job of a dedicated Cheer Squad member is to spread school spirit wherever she or he goes — to boost morale for all school competitors?"

She nodded. "I would say that's the ultimate goal — yes. Very insightful of you."

"So whenever we're at a school event, we should do our best to boost morale, right?"

"Of course."

"Thanks, Coach Manbeck. This talk has been very enlightening."

"Glad I could help."

After she walked off, I continued to scan the big calendar. This being a small town, there weren't a whole lot of sports in our middle school, and out of what we did have, much of it hadn't gotten going yet. In fact, it looked to be all football — football practices, football boosters, football games. I was about to give up when I noticed an entry on this coming Saturday — a cross-country meet at a nearby park.

"Perfect," I said to myself. A good feeling washed over me, making me smile and skip back over to Darby. This was the best mood I'd been in since school started. I now had a plan to change things for the better, and that was going to make seventh grade all the more bearable — perhaps even enjoyable.

I rushed back to my small group, interrupting what they were doing.

"Hey, Riley and Aurelia, we're going to do some bonus cheering. Do you want to join us?"

"Bonus cheering?" Aurelia looked over at Riley, who shrugged. Then they both looked at Darby.

"It's a . . . special project of ours," Darby said.

"Yeah," I said. "To stop the rampant discrimination against less popular forms of sports and make Cheer Squad more egalitarian. It'll be fun!"

"Um . . . maybe," Riley said. "So what would we have to do?"

"Basically just show up where we tell you and cheer when you get there," I said.

Darby peered at me closely. "Dawn? Is Coach Manbeck okay with this?"

"Not to worry. I've already cleared it with her," I said with a wave of my pom-pom. Then I turned to Riley and Aurelia. "Wanna join our cause?"

"I guess so."

"Excellent. So what are you doing on Saturday about six a.m.?"

CHAPTER THIRTEEN

Evasive Maneuvers

Darby

On Friday, Wanda wore really cool shoes. I knew this because I kept ducking under my desk. They were dark blue lace-up boots with little yellow lightning bolts all over them. I was glad she wore them. It made my view a lot less boring while I was stooped over.

The reason I was hunched over all the time was because Mrs. Champion kept scanning the class and asking people to share their thoughts aloud. She would talk about something in the textbook and say, "Who wants to volunteer their opinion?" Then when no one raised his or her hand, she would glance around the room and call on the person her gaze landed on.

That didn't seem like volunteering to me.

I figured as long as she couldn't see me, she'd never choose me. So I always managed to be tying my shoes, picking up a pen I "accidentally" dropped, or digging something out of my backpack whenever she started searching for the next person.

Thankfully, my strategy was working. I'd managed to avoid Mrs. Champion's eye all through class, and there were only a few minutes left before the bell rang. Although my back was getting stiff and sore from being bent over so much.

"So the Karankawa people all had two names. One was only known by close family. Do any of you have special nicknames that your family gave you? Anyone want to share?"

Doppy. I smiled down at the carpet, remembering. When we were really little, Delaney was the first triplet who started talking. She could say Dawn well enough, but she called me Doppy. I don't remember it — I just remember my parents and Lily talking about it and sometimes calling me that when they were being silly. I always thought it sounded like a name for a magical elf.

No way was I going to volunteer all that, though. I'd almost gotten through the whole class without getting noticed and planned to keep my streak going. Besides, Tucker would laugh at my Doppy story and then he'd go off and tell his friend Rowdy Buchanan and soon everyone would be calling me that.

"Anyone?" Mrs. Champion asked.

I scooched even lower and tried to forget the twinge in my back by admiring Wanda's shoes again.

Soon I spied another pair of footwear. They were maroon-colored flats and they were walking right toward me. I knew

they belonged to Mrs. Champion. Like an opossum playing dead, I stayed real still. But it was no use — the shoes
kept coming and coming until they stopped right in front of
my desk.

"Darby Brewster? Are you back there? We haven't heard
from you yet. Maybe you should volunteer to take this topic."

I made a face because I knew she didn't mean volunteer
like I could say "no thank you." Since I was all hunkered
over, Mrs. Champion couldn't see me grimace. But Wanda
could.

"Mrs. Champion?" Wanda was waving her hand in the
air. Suddenly I worried she would tell the teacher I was hiding and secretly making faces. Instead she said, "Darby's not
feeling well."

"She isn't?"

"No. She told me so when she came in, and she's been all
folded over like that ever since. I think it's a virus."

"Is she going to throw up?" someone asked.

"Eww!" someone else said.

Then Tucker started trying to scoot his desk away from
me, saying, "I don't want to be in the line of fire."

I groaned. This was the kind of negative attention I was
trying to avoid, and it was maybe even worse than people
knowing about Doppy.

"Darby? Let me see you," Mrs. Champion said. "I'm
worried."

I slowly sat up straight. Everyone was staring at me.

Luckily, all that embarrassment, plus keeping my head low for half an hour, had made my face go red. I could feel the tingly warmth in my cheeks. Mrs. Champion put her hand on my forehead and said, "My goodness, you do look sick." Her face looked so kind and concerned that I almost told her the truth. But I was still too shy to talk. All I could do was nod back.

Luckily, the bell rang right at that moment, and everyone stopped looking at me and began packing up their things. Mrs. Champion said, "Why don't you go straight to the nurse, Darby. I sure hope you feel better soon."

As I headed into the hallway, I saw Wanda standing there. She fell into step beside me.

"Hi," she said.

"Hi," I said back. "Um . . . thanks, for . . ." I wasn't sure how to phrase it. Thanks for lying for me? Thanks for helping me avoid being called on?

Before I could decide how to phrase it, she smiled at me and said, "No problem. So tell me. How come you never want to answer questions?"

Now my cheeks felt like they were on fire. "I . . . I just . . . I'm shy. It's hard for me to speak up."

"Yeah, I thought so. It's hard for me, too. I'm not as shy as you, but still. It's tough because no one knows who I am yet."

I glanced over at her. Wanda walked slightly humpbacked, with her big black backpack slung behind her and her hands in her front pockets. Her eyes, what I could see of them, kept glancing around at the people passing us and the posters on the walls. I tried to imagine how she must be feeling. I had no idea what it was like to walk through a school and not know anyone there — mainly because I've lived in the same small town my whole life and knew most of the kids in my grade even before I started school. But I figured it probably didn't feel good.

I thought about what Mrs. Neighbor had said to me when I dove behind her nandina bushes. Taking a deep breath, I said, "Wanda, I have to tell you something."

"Really? What?" She seemed surprised. We stopped walking and stood against the wall, near the trophy case.

"I . . . I . . ." I took another big breath and forced the rest of the sentence out of me. "I was the one who left the bag on your front step that one day."

"*You're* the Pop-Tart Fairy?" Wanda smiled so big, the tips of her cheeks disappeared behind her bangs.

"I was trying to do something nice to welcome you to the neighborhood."

"It was nice. I love Pop-Tarts. But why didn't you ring the doorbell and say hi? Is it because of the shyness?"

I nodded and stared down at my shoes.

"Well, now I can say thank you. So, thank you!"

"You're welcome."

"I hope you come by my house again sometime. Only this time, I hope you ring the bell."

"I promise I will."

"Good."

The blaze in my cheeks had gone out and I felt much less shy. In fact, I felt great. I hadn't known Wanda that long, but already she knew personal things about me — like my shyness and how I was hiding from the teacher. But instead of feeling ashamed, I felt closer to her.

"By the way, you have the coolest shoes," I said.

"Thanks."

"And the coolest haircut."

"Thanks."

"And the second coolest bicycle."

"Second coolest?"

All the way to her second period I told her about Lucas Westbrook, the rich boy who lived down the street from us, and his beautiful silver bike. I was almost late to my own class because of it, but I didn't mind. I'd made a friend.

And walking the halls with a friend felt almost as good as walking with sisters.

CHAPTER FOURTEEN

Primary Race

Delaney

Where is everyone?" Mom asked as she pulled the car into Scofield Park.

The place did seem pretty empty. Probably because the sun hadn't come up yet and most people were home in bed, or, like our mom was just twenty minutes ago, stumbling around their houses with a cup of coffee. In the dim light, we could eventually see a cluster of people near the swing sets.

"Over there!" Dawn said, pointing.

Mom pulled up near the playground area, and sure enough, we could see that the assembled people were wearing running outfits in many different colors. One group clearly had on navy blue JCMS shirts, the same color as the Pom Squad shirts we had on. After putting the car in park, Mom turned to look at us. Her face was still a little puffy like it gets when she first wakes up, and her hair hadn't been brushed yet. "You sure you have whatever it is you need?"

"Let's see . . ." Dawn said. "Pom-poms — check. Megaphone — check. Three water bottles — check. Yep. All set."

"Here." Mom pulled her cell phone out of her purse and handed it to Darby. "Call my office phone when you're done and I'll come pick you up."

"Wow, thanks, Mom," I said. She smiled and then it turned into a yawn.

"And thanks for driving us here so early," Darby said.

"You're welcome," Mom said. "I'm just happy you girls are enjoying Pom Squad. Although, I have to say, it sure has changed over the years. I don't think they ever cheered for cross-country when I was in school."

"Actually —" I began.

"Actually, we really should get up there and get ready," Dawn interrupted. "Thanks, Mom! Bye!"

We climbed out of the car with our gear and waved to Mom. By now, more cars were starting to pull into the lot. We fell into step behind three girl runners wearing yellow-and-green outfits and joined the small crowd congregating nearby.

Even with all the practicing over the summer and a couple of weeks of getting up early for school, Darby was still zonked that morning. I had to help steer her through the park so she didn't bump into trees. Dawn, on the other hand, seemed wide awake. In fact, she was all fired up and barking out orders.

Dawn stood with her hands on her hips, surveying the surroundings. "Where are Riley and Aurelia and all the other recruits?" she asked. "Didn't we remind them?"

"Yeah, but . . . I don't think they're coming," Darby said. "Aurelia said she thought she was busy."

"That's crazy. Who has plans at six a.m. on a Saturday?" Dawn said, throwing her arms up.

"Exactly," Darby said. "That means she doesn't want to come. And I'm guessing it's the same with Riley. And probably the others we talked to don't want to come, either."

Dawn made a huffing sound. "What kind of spirit leaders are they?"

"Probably the kind who want to sleep in on a Saturday," I said.

"Fine," Dawn said. "We don't need them. One nice thing about being a triplet is that you have your own built-in group."

"Where do you think we should stand and cheer?" I asked, glancing all around.

"Probably near that banner that says 'Start,'" Dawn said, pointing.

There were probably four different girls' cross-country teams there, all of them stretching and talking in the same general area. After stashing our supplies under a nearby tree, we found an open spot in front of them and stood at attention, pom-poms in hand, hands on hips.

A woman walked over to us. I knew she was the coach because she had on a JCMS T-shirt that said COACH across the back.

"Excuse me, are you three with the team?"

"We're official Cheer Squad people and we're here to cheer our team on," I explained.

"Is that so?" she said, her eyebrows flying high on her forehead. "Well, okay, I guess. But you're standing on the actual course. We need to keep this area right here clear, all right?"

"Yes, ma'am. We will," Dawn said, and we scooted over to the side.

After she walked away, Dawn leaned in toward me and said, "I think it's time to get started. Why don't you lead us, Delaney? You have the loudest voice." That was the first time someone had pointed that out in a good way.

We spaced ourselves out, and then I cupped my hands around my mouth and started a cheer. *"Hey, hey, it's time to fight!"* Suddenly I felt Darby elbowing me in my side.

"Um, Delaney," she said. "That's for football. Running isn't a contact sport."

"Oh yeah. How about this? *Hey, fans in the stands!*" More elbows — this time from Dawn. Only she didn't have to explain why she stopped me. "Right. No stands." It sure would have been easier if there were stands. Everyone was kind of milling about and it was hard to know how to face the crowd.

Eventually we just stood in a row, facing the area marked off as the running path. Dawn glanced over at me and nodded. This time I decided to do a simple chant of our school initials.

"J! C! M! S!" Clap! "J! C! M! S!" Clap! "J! C! M! S!" Darby joined up with me, stomping and clapping. I think she was cheering, too, but I couldn't hear her over my own voice. Meanwhile, Dawn was chanting through the megaphone.

After a couple of rounds, a few other onlookers joined in. It was amazing! Dawn caught my eye and gave me a thumbs-up. We continued the chant three more times and then I ended it with some spirited whooping and clapping.

Two of the yellow-and-green-wearing runners walked past as we were taking sips of water. I heard one girl say to the other, "Hey, how come only their team has cheerleaders?" This made us smile again.

At that point, the runners seemed to be done stretching and they all stood in a clumpy semicircle by the starting line. Dawn gave me the signal to start us again, and this time I decided to just make up a cheer for cross-country — one that got right to the point. "Go, Patriots! Go, Patriots! Run run run! Go, Patriots! Go, Patriots! Run run run!"

We repeated it three times, and in the middle of the fourth time, a man in a white cap fired off the starting gun. It was so loud, I screamed and stopped the cheer.

Instantly the runners took off. We hollered and jumped up and down, and I even did a couple of cartwheels as soon as there was room, which felt great. Strangely, most of the runners didn't even look at us, they just focused straight ahead. But a couple of them smiled.

We watched as they ran down the stretch and up a little rise. Once they'd all disappeared behind a grove of trees, we stopped our whooping and hollering.

"Yes!" Dawn said, raising her fist in the air. "Good job, team."

"That was fun!" I said, giving Darby a high five.

"So now what?" Darby asked.

"We wait, I guess," Dawn said. "Keep a lookout for when they return."

"How long will that be?" I asked.

Dawn shrugged. "Maybe you should ask someone. I'm going to grab a sip of water."

As she and Darby headed back to our tree, I turned to a lady walking past. "Excuse me, ma'am. About how long until the runners head back here?"

She gave me a funny look. "What are you talking about?"

"The runners who just ran off. How long until they return?"

"They don't. This is cross-country, not track. They run *across country*. Instead of a loop, the path is a line."

My mouth dropped open. I'm not sure why I never understood that before. It was right there in the name, all along.

I ran over to Dawn and Darby. "Um, I have some bad news. Those runners? They aren't coming back here. Ever." I explained to them about cross-country.

"Huh." Dawn tapped her finger against her chin. "Well, that's a detail we probably shouldn't have overlooked."

"Wait . . ." Darby held up one hand like a traffic cop. "So that's it? We got up before the sun and came all the way out here to boost spirit for five minutes?"

"Guess so." Dawn's voice was the opposite of cheering.

I was disappointed, too. Not only had it been fun, it was also good to see Dawn excited about cheering. If this project of hers went well, she might change her mind about Cheer Squad.

"So what's happening now? Where's everyone going?" Darby pointed to the parking lot, where all the coaches and onlookers were getting into cars and driving away.

"I don't know, but I'm going to find out," Dawn said, and walked over to chat with the same coach from before. After a while she came back

"What are they doing?" I asked.

"They're driving to the finish line — which, if you ask me, doesn't seem like setting a good example for your runners," Dawn said. "Anyway, I asked them if we could go with them and cheer at the end of the race."

"Great idea!"

"Unfortunately, there was no room in her car because of all the big coolers and other people. Plus, she said something about liability."

"Oh."

"But there was also good news. She said another reason they had to leave was because the boys' team has their meet right here in an hour, so they had to clear out for them."

"We can stay here and cheer for them!" I said, jumping up and down.

"And we can be even more prepared," Dawn said. "There's got to be a better way to do this. Ideas?"

I twirled in a circle a few times until a good idea spun up in my head. "Okay, I got it," I said as I stopped turning. Then I waited a few seconds for the rest of the park to stop spinning. "What if we spaced ourselves out at various spots around the course? That way they could kind of get cheered the whole way."

"Hmmm . . ." Dawn tapped her finger against her chin. "But that would have just one of us cheering for a whole area. Wouldn't it be kind of quiet? Darby would probably be too shy anyway."

"I would," Darby said. "I can't deny it."

"But it is a good idea, Delaney," Dawn said, patting me on

my shoulder. "We'll do it for the next meet, when we have more Cheer Squad people joining us." Darby and I exchanged looks. I could tell she felt the same way I did — that we probably weren't going to convince anyone else to join us at a park at six a.m. on a Saturday.

"Also," Dawn went on, "next time we can make spirit signs to hang in the trees. Or maybe bring the drum line. I sure wish we could get hold of a T-shirt cannon. That would help fire things up."

I giggled. "Ha! Fire things up. I get it!" Dawn just frowned at me, though, so I guess she didn't mean it as a joke. Once again, Darby and I traded looks. But not for long, because just then a couple of cars pulled up and another coach got out. I recognized him from school.

"Any other ideas?" Dawn asked. She waited a full minute, and when neither Darby nor I said anything else, said, "Fine. We'll just do the best we can. But let me know if you get any flashes of brilliance."

As we waited for the next race, Darby pumped herself forward and back on a nearby swing, Dawn sat on a bench tapping her chin and muttering, and I did a little of everything — slides, swings, monkey bars. Soon the boys and their coaching staffs started to show up. When it seemed like most everyone had arrived, Dawn stood up from the bench and motioned to us.

"Places, everyone!" Dawn yelled.

Only none of us were sure what places she meant, so we went in different directions for a couple of moments. Finally we arranged ourselves near our previous cheer spot, where all the teams were assembling for a prerace stretch. As I glanced over at the runners, I noticed a familiar face. "Hey, look, there's Tommy Ybarra," I said to Dawn and Darby. "Tommy! Hi! Hey, Tommy!"

Tommy glanced around, looking confused. Eventually he saw us standing over to the side.

"Run fast, Tommy!" I said, jumping up and down. Other runners were looking at him now. They were probably jealous that he had three official spirit boosters cheering him on.

A really tall man in JCMS colors came over to us, the boys' coach from our school. "What's going on?" he asked.

"We're here to officially cheer on the JCMS runners," Dawn said. "We just gave the girls' team a great send-off."

Coach took off his cap and scratched his head. "Well, all right. But be careful to stay out of the way, okay?"

"You have our word, Coach!" Dawn said. After he walked back to his team, she turned to me. "Go ahead and get started. I think they're almost ready."

"Aye-aye," I said, saluting her with a pom-pom.

I decided to lead us in the "Our Team Is Red Hot" cheer, which was really appropriate because the sun was up now and everyone was looking kind of pink and sweaty.

"*Our team is red hot!*" I began. Dawn and Darby joined me on the next part. "*Our team is red hot! Our team is R-E-D H-O-T. Once we start, we can't stop!*" Clap! Clap!

The runners and onlookers reacted pretty much the same as the group before — some confused, others smiling — but this time, no one joined in with us. When we finished, there was a little trickle of applause.

For the next cheer, I did another made-up cross-country chant: "*We've got spirit, we've got force, we've got the best runners on the course!*" It took a couple of rounds, but eventually Dawn and Darby joined in. When we finished this one, the clapping was even louder and there were more smiles. It really did feel like we were boosting spirit.

Just as we were about to start another cheer, an official shouted for the runners to get ready.

"Good job, Delaney," Darby said as we stood silently, waiting for the starting gun.

"Yeah," Dawn said. "If only we could somehow keep it up throughout the race."

And right at that moment, I got a good idea — a way to keep the cheering going. It popped into my brain just as the starting gun went off. The only downside was, there was no time to bring it up with Dawn and Darby. I had to test this one out on my own.

Since there were so many runners, they all had to start out kind of slowish, so it was easy for me to scoot along the sidelines with them. I scanned the faces and eventually found Tommy Ybarra. Tommy wasn't exactly a friend of ours, but we liked him fine. And my idea would work best if I fixed on only one of the racers.

"Go, Tommy, go!" I shouted as I sidestepped beside the crowd of runners. "Go, Tommy, go!"

I continued to run alongside him, calling out the cheer. I couldn't do any jumps, though, because I was running. Soon the pack started going faster, but this was when I tested out the main part of my plan: I put on a burst of speed and ran way out in front of Tommy on the side of the course. When he got near me again, I started jumping and shouting his name again.

"*TOM-my! TOM-my! TOM-my! TOM-my!*"

"What are you doing?" he said as he went past.

"Cheering!" I was having so much fun, I decided to do it some more. I put on another burst of speed, ran out way ahead of him, and hollered and jumped for him all over again.

"Stop it!" he said as he passed me again. Only I didn't really pay attention to what he was saying at the time, because I was enjoying myself too much.

I raced far ahead to another spot along the course and chanted his name a third time.

"Go away!" Tommy said as he ran past, this time a little more loudly. Then he scrunched up his face, ducked his head, and started running really fast. I tried, but I couldn't catch up to him.

I stood and watched as he disappeared into the distance. And then I realized something: Tommy was way far ahead of the other runners.

"Wow," I said to myself. "This cheerleading thing really works!"

CHAPTER FIFTEEN

Situation Room

Dawn

I just don't understand. Who told you to go out and cheer?"

It was Monday morning at school and we were in Mr. Plunkett's office with Coach Manbeck, the two cross-country coaches, and of course Mr. Plunkett. I'd noticed he'd added another chair, facing his desk, so my sisters and I could all sit now. But that meant the coaches were all standing behind him, like a very tall, very stern wall.

"Well . . ." Delaney glanced over at me. "No one told us to. It was kind of our own idea."

"We thought it would be nice to boost spirit for other athletic events," Darby added, "and would make things more fair."

Everything went silent while the adults exchanged glances.

"Are we in trouble?" I asked. "Because I know my rights. We're not saying anything more until we know what we're being charged with — at the risk of being self-incriminating."

"No," said Coach Manbeck, "you aren't in trouble. I for one think it's great that you wanted to spread school spirit. It was a very bold and original idea. It's just that you should have told me first."

I tilted my head. "But I did mention it to you," I said. "You agreed that it was our duty as Cheer Squad members to boost spirit at all school events."

"Oh, that." Coach Manbeck looked over at Mr. Plunkett. "It's true. I did agree to that sentiment."

"The problem is," said the girls' cross-country coach, "there are reasons why our sport doesn't typically have Cheer Squads out at the racing site. There are safety issues, for one."

"Like snakes?" Delaney asked.

"Poison ivy?" Darby asked.

"Misfiring T-shirt cannons?" I asked.

The coach kept shaking her head no. "I mean, like what if one of you had fallen and gotten hurt?"

Darby, Delaney, and I met one another's eyes. We knew about such mishaps. "Right," I said. "I guess we didn't think about that."

"But also," said the boys' coach, "my runners need to focus, and all the yelling and jumping is a distraction. Plus, shouting at them to go faster goes against coaching advice. Cross-country races are not sprints. If they go too fast, they won't have enough energy left to finish the race. Tommy Ybarra barely finished on Saturday."

"Oh no." Delaney's voice cracked slightly. "I'm sorry. I just wanted to fill him with the fire of champions."

The boys' coach smiled. "It's all right. This was just a practice meet, and now Tommy knows the importance of reserving energy. But I hope you understand that we can't have you out there cheering for us like that."

"But you're definitely welcome to come watch," added the girls' coach. "Or even join the team."

I noticed Delaney and Darby perk up a bit, as if seriously considering that. It was time for me to take charge.

I cleared my throat and stood up from my chair. "On behalf of my sisters and me, I just want to say that we're sorry. All we wanted was for *all* of the athletes to feel special — not just a select few. The way we see it, everyone deserves a chance to shine at something."

The girls' coach stepped forward and held out her hand. I shook it. "I think it's great that the three of you wanted to boost school spirit at additional events," she said. "But cross-country just isn't the best fit."

"You have our word, ma'am," I said. "We won't cheer for cross-country anymore."

"Good. I appreciate that," said the boys' cross-country coach.

At that point, Mr. Plunkett thanked all three coaches for

their time and said that they could go, that he would handle it the rest of the way.

"Coach Manbeck," Delaney said, her voice still a little shaky, "are we kicked out of Cheer Squad?"

"No. Of course not."

"And you still take the position that spirit boosting is for the whole school and not just the select few?" I asked.

"I do," Coach Manbeck said. "Thank you for trying." She gave me a little pat on the back as she went past and then headed out into the hallway behind the other coaches.

After the coaches left, Mr. Plunkett took off his glasses and looked each of us in the eye. "I'm glad we were all able to straighten that out," he said. "Do any of you want to stay longer and talk about what happened?"

"Not really."

"No."

Darby shook her head.

"Very well, then. Here are passes for each of you to head back to class. You may go." Mr. Plunkett handed each of us a small pink slip of paper. Then he put his glasses back on and turned toward his computer.

We headed out into the corridor and shut the door behind us. "Wow," Delaney said. "Did you count how many adults were in there? It was like the Situation Room in the White House."

"I know," Darby said. "I feel so ashamed."

"What are you talking about?" I said. "We didn't get in any trouble. Did you hear what Coach Manbeck said?" I could still feel the spot on my back where she gave me a pat. "I think she was trying to send us a message."

Darby made a face. "A message? What kind of message?"

"That she wants us to keep trying to boost spirit for less popular activities. We just chose the wrong sport, is all."

"I'm not sure that's what she meant," Delaney said.

"Sure it was. We just have to have a better plan next time."

"So . . . there'll be a next time?" Darby asked.

Only I didn't get to answer, because right at that moment Delaney started shouting. "Look, there's Lucas. Hey, Lucas! Over here!"

Sure enough, Lucas Westbrook was standing on a step stool, taping up a sign on the wall. He glanced over and smiled a shiny smile at us. He got his braces off just last month, but his smile still gleams. Plus, I noticed he'd gotten taller since the last time we saw him.

"Hi, Lucas. What are you doing?" Delaney said as she scurried up to him, with Darby and me a few steps behind.

"Hanging up some posters," Lucas said. "What are you guys doing?"

"We were just talking with Mr. Plunkett again," I said.

"Again?" Lucas looked confused.

"Yeah, we pretty much talk to him on a regular basis now," Delaney explained, "on account of we're still trying to get into Color Guard."

"We're in Cheer Squad instead," I said.

"But only because we were hungry for corn dogs," Delaney said.

"We're trying to make the best of it," Darby said.

Lucas stepped down off the stool and turned to face us. "Do y'all want to come over after school? I got some cool new stuff."

Lucas is just about the most spoiled boy in Texas. I'm not joking. You know all the gadgets, gizmos, and games that regular kids tend to have? Well, Lucas has the best, most expensive kinds. And usually five of them. Plus, he has all kinds of extra things that no one has — like his own golf cart and an actual machine that can make soda pop however you like it.

But Lucas is also really nice and a reliable friend. He always shares and likes it when people come over. Over the summer, he tried to teach us how to lasso, and he never got annoyed when we knocked things over or scared his cat, Megamuffin, or lassoed the sprinkler and accidentally made it spray water onto the grill, soaking our hamburgers, like Delaney did once.

Also, Lucas has nice eyes. They're such a pretty color blue that when I look at them, I sometimes forget what I'm talking about. That's why I was staring at his sneakers instead.

"Sorry, we can't join you," I said to his shoes. "We have an important meeting tonight." We actually didn't have one officially scheduled yet, but I figured we probably would, since we needed to figure out where to cheer next.

"Oh, okay," Lucas said. "Maybe later on, then."

"Sure."

"Well, gotta go finish hanging these up. Bye!"

Once Lucas was a few yards away and I couldn't see his eyes anymore, my mind worked better. That's when a new thought occurred to me. "Hey, Lucas," I called out.

He turned around. "Yeah?"

"Do you have a T-shirt cannon, by any chance?"

He tilted his head, no doubt considering his vast treasure of toys, tools, and other doohickeys. "No," he said finally.

"Too bad," I said. "Think your folks would get you one if you asked?"

"Huh?"

"Dawn!" Darby whisper-yelled.

"Never mind," I called back to Lucas. "Carry on with what you're doing. Go . . ." I glanced up at the poster he'd just hung on the wall: JCMS CHESS CLUB MATCH — 7:00 P.M. MONDAY IN THE CAFETERIA. "Go chess club!"

"Thanks," he said, and kept on walking.

Go chess club. My words seem to echo inside my head. Go . . . chess . . . club. And just like that, a brilliant plan lit up my brain like fireworks. I stood there openmouthed, my hand still raised in a wave. By the time Lucas had disappeared around the corner, I knew what we had to do.

"Darby? Delaney? Come in close," I said, waving them toward me. "I have another idea. An even better one."

"What's going on?" Delaney asked.

"Our goal of spreading spirit can still be achieved. What we need to do" — I paused for suspense and looked each of them in the eye — "is cheer for people who don't even get the honor of being called athletes."

CHAPTER SIXTEEN

Oh Say, Can You See

Darby

Our house was full of noise. Mom was meeting with a client somewhere in town, and we stayed at home so we could walk over to the school for the seven p.m. chess meet. In the meantime, Dawn was upstairs playing with the megaphone she had borrowed, and Delaney was in the living room testing out cheers for tonight's spirit booster. Quincy, meanwhile, thought Delaney was playing with him and kept running all around, whining and barking. It's times like these when our house feels really small, and I can't seem to find a room — or even a corner — where I can just sit and ponder.

I went outside, sat down on the steps of our porch, and tried to sort out my thoughts — but it was hard. I'd be thinking about Mrs. Champion's class and how I might avoid her calling on me, and then I'd hear Dawn's voice through the open window of our bedroom, bugling through the megaphone: "We hold these truths to be self-evident: that all men and women are created equal . . ." Or I'd be trying to decide how I felt about Dawn's big idea to cheer for chess team, but then I'd hear Delaney jumping around the living room, hollering, *"We are challenged! And challenged we will be!"*

After a while, I got up and walked over to the flagpole in the middle of our front yard. I placed my hand on its smooth metal surface, still warm from the sun, and twirled around and around, faster and faster — the way Delaney likes to do. She says moving around helps her brain think, kind of like shaking a pan of muddy gravel to find a chunk of gold. Unfortunately, all it did was make me dizzy.

Feeling woozy, I sat on the concrete base and leaned against the pole. As I waited to feel steady again, I saw something coming toward me. It took me a minute to figure out what it was, because I was still all whirly and the image kept sliding off to the right.

"Hi," said the swirly figure.

I blinked my eyes several times. Eventually my eyes focused and I could see Wanda standing in front of me, smiling. Her pretty aqua-colored bicycle was leaning against our fence at the end of our driveway.

"Hi there," I said.

"I was riding past and saw you sitting out here, so I thought I'd come over," she said. "If that's okay."

"Of course." I got to my feet and brushed dirt off my shorts. "Do you want to . . ." I paused. I had been about to invite her inside, but it was so loud. Dawn was now reciting Kennedy's inaugural address and Delaney was whooping and, from the sound of it, jumping all over the room.

Plus, for some reason, I didn't want to share her with Dawn and Delaney — at least not yet. I figured I had some time before our chess meet cheering.

"Do you want to go for a walk?" I said finally. "I can show you some cool places."

She smiled. "Okay. Can I leave my bike here?"

"Sure."

As we headed out of the yard, I noticed a gray, square-shaped bag hanging across her body. "What's that?" I asked, pointing.

"It's my camera. I take it pretty much everywhere with me."

"Why?"

"To keep a record of the Now."

"The Now?"

Wanda laughed nervously. "Yeah. It's kind of hard to explain. You'll think I'm weird."

"I promise I won't."

She unzipped her bag, pulled out a camera, and hooked the strap around her neck. "It's like . . . most people are in a different time," she said, taking off the lens cap. "They're either worrying about the future or mulling over something that happened in the past. But when I take a photo" — she lifted the camera and clicked a picture of me — "I'm right here, right now. It helps me appreciate things better." She paused while I considered. "See? Told you it would sound silly."

"But it doesn't." I shook my head. "It sounds wise. Come on. Let me show you some more Now."

Wanda followed me down Nugent Avenue, past Mr. Neighbor who was watering his crepe myrtles and shouted, "Make way for ducklings!" at us, and on toward the center of town. Occasionally she'd stop, lift her camera, and take a picture of a lizard on a fence post or a dried-up creek bed, but mainly she just walked beside me, looking intently at everything around us. I enjoyed the silence. After a while, though, I got curious and started up more conversation.

"So where did you move from?" I asked.

"San Antonio."

"Were you sad to leave?"

She shrugged. "A little. But my mom really needed a job and it was stressful not having enough money. She was so happy when she got the job at the bank here. She's happier, so I'm happier. Besides, my dad is still in San Antonio, so I get to visit there a lot."

"Your parents are divorced?"

She nodded. "Since I was three."

"Mine are divorced, too. Since I was nine. Do you have brothers or sisters?"

"Nope, it's just me and my mom. When I visit my dad, it's just me and my dad."

"Wow, your houses must be nice and quiet."

Wanda smiled. "I guess they are. I usually think it's boring, though."

I shook my head in wonder. I couldn't imagine a house with just two people living in it. When you had to make a decision, there would just be one person you had to agree with. When you had to share, there would just be one person to share with. If something ended up missing, and you know you didn't take it, you'd automatically know who did.

"I have three sisters," I said as Wanda stopped to take a picture of an old faded sign for a winery. "One is a lot older, Lily — she's twenty-three. Another is older than me by seven minutes. That's Dawn. Delaney is the youngest. She was born ten minutes after I was."

"One of your sisters is in my math class," she said. "I thought she was you at first."

"Does she get up to sharpen her pencil a lot?"

"Yeah. How'd you know?"

"That's how you can tell it's Delaney."

"I wondered why you were so shy in history class but talked all the time in math." Wanda stopped walking and looked at me. "I'm sorry. Was that a rude thing to say? I imagine people get you guys mixed up a lot. I bet that's annoying."

I shrugged. "Only sometimes. People who really know us can tell us apart. I'm sure you'll be able to soon."

Her grin came back.

We were now heading into the main part of town. The workday was ending, so there was more traffic than usual and we had to be extra careful crossing the streets.

"That's the library," I said, pointing. "And see this oak tree? Delaney got stuck up on that limb when she was six. She pitched a real racket, too. Screamed so loud, she woke up Reverend Hoffmeyer, who was napping in his office." I nodded toward our church down the road. "He was the one who ran over and helped talk her down. I remember there was a big crowd of people watching, and Dawn and I were standing over there, bawling. A man even took a picture and put it in the paper. We have a clipping of it back home. We wanted Mom to frame it and hang it on the wall, but she said no. She said it wasn't our finest moment."

Wanda walked all around the tree, her head tilted to the side. Eventually she stopped, raised her camera, and took a couple of pictures.

"What's that over there?" She pointed down the street to a pretty clapboard building with a long porch.

"Oh, that's Ever's — only we always call it *Forever's* on account of how old it is and how it never changes. It has the

123

best pies in town — all kinds, like pecan, blueberry, lemon chiffon . . ."

"Which one's your favorite?"

"Well . . ." I looked down and lifted one shoulder. "I usually get the one that hasn't been ordered as much. Because . . ." I broke off, suddenly feeling foolish.

"Because you feel sorry for it?" Wanda asked. I glanced up, my eyes probably as big as pie pans. As I studied her face, I realized she wasn't making fun of me. "Yeah," I said. "How did you know?"

She shrugged. "I guess because I do things like that, too."

Wanda and I were sharing secrets. I'd never revealed things like that to someone outside of my family. I wasn't sure if it should make me feel guilty or not — but it didn't. It actually felt great. Amazing, even.

"You know," Wanda began as she raised her camera and focused on Ever's, "when we were adopting our cat at the shelter, everyone wanted the cute kittens. But I picked Mariposa, a grown-up cat that no one was looking at. On her card it said that she'd belonged to this man who was very old and died. I felt bad for her. We took her home, and you know what? She's been the best. We didn't have to litter box train her or teach her not to scratch. And when she comes to sit on my lap, she first touches her nose to mine. I think it's her way of saying thank you for getting her out of that sad place."

"That's so sweet."

I couldn't believe someone felt the same way I did. It was like finding another sister — one who wasn't like me on the outside, but was an exact duplicate on the inside.

We turned a corner and went down another street, one close to the town square. The sun was hiding behind trees and buildings, making colors darker and shadows longer. There was even a nice breeze. It seemed like our little town was trying to present itself at its best for Wanda's sake, and I said a silent thank you to it.

"Do you want to try?" Wanda said, holding the camera out to me.

I lifted one of my shoulders in a shy shrug. I did want to, but I was afraid. "What if I mess it up?"

"What's to mess up? You just look through there and press this button. Just like on your cell phone."

"I don't have a cell phone."

"But you do know how to press buttons, right?"

"Yes. But . . . what do I take pictures of?"

"Anything." She opened her arms and gestured all about. "It's up to you. That's what's cool about photography. You can put a bunch of photographers in the same place, but they'll focus on different things. I guess because we're all different and see the world in different ways."

At first I was afraid I might accidentally drop the camera or do something wrong. But after a while I really enjoyed it. It made me notice things I hadn't seen before — like the birds nesting in the blocky U-shape of the Union Motors sign, and a pretty stained-glass window in an old building. I even noticed a cloud shaped like a lobster.

"Ooh, donuts," Wanda said. We were coming up on another old building, with the words DAISY'S DONUTS over the door.

"Oh yeah. Hey! I think I know someone here," I said, spotting a familiar face behind the counter. "Let's go inside."

"Hi, Bree!" I greeted. Her blue eyes were lined in dark black, and her lips were painted a burgundy color.

"Hi yourself. Who's this?"

"This is Wanda. She's new."

"Nice to meet you, Wanda. I like your hair."

"Thanks. I like yours, too."

Bree usually dyes her hair crazy colors. Most of it was pulled back in a bun and she had on a light brown visor, but the bangs that hung down her forehead were bright purple.

"So are you back at school?" Bree asked.

"Yep."

"Did Lily and Alex finally tie the knot this summer?"

"No, there was too much going on. But they're probably going to get married this fall." We sat at a table near the counter and I explained to Wanda about my older sister and her fiancé, and how Bree and I met when she was a bridesmaid at Lily's Almost Wedding to a guy named Burton. Meanwhile Bree gave us a box of different-flavored donut holes that she refused to let us pay for, saying they were one day old and supposed to be thrown away — even if they were still really good.

"So where are the other triplets?" Bree asked me.

I shrugged. "Doing other stuff. We're supposed to meet up later and . . . Wait. What time is it?"

"Seven fifteen."

I stood up from the table, gasping loudly. "Oh no. I'm late!"

CHAPTER SEVENTEEN

Board of Regulation

Delaney

Where is she?" Dawn asked for the forty-seventh time.

I shrugged for the forty-seventh time.

"This is a disgrace. A total fiasco! Blowing off your comrades is rude and unprofessional. If Darby were a member of my cabinet, she'd be booted for this."

"I thought for sure she'd already be here, waiting for us," I said. "Maybe she's just running a little late? You know we can rely on her." It occurred to me that in Darby's absence, I was taking on her role of keeping things positive.

"Well, no matter what, we go ahead with the plan," Dawn said. "We're here for a reason. These people need us."

The cafeteria was about half full. Chessboards were set out, two on each long table. At the front of the room was a big whiteboard on a stand with a list of last names paired up with each other. I recognized a few of the kids, and Mr. Langerham, my math teacher from last year, was standing out in the hallway talking with another grown-up. There was a buzzy sense of anticipation in the air, just like at the pep rally and before the cross-country races. It reminded me of the countdown on New Year's Eve, only I wasn't sleepy — in fact, I felt just the opposite.

"Hey, guys!" Lucas walked toward us, all smiles. He looked happy to see us.

I thought Dawn would be happy to see him, too, but as he came near, she just looked down at her shoes.

"I didn't know you were coming," he said. "Did you want to play chess?"

"Even better — we're here to cheer on all the players!" I said, hopping on my toes.

"It's not fair that football and basketball are the only sports that get rallies and cheers and other spirit boosts," Dawn explained. "You all are also competitors, so you deserve people making a big fuss, too."

"So we're here to make a big fuss!" I raised my arms and shook the silver pom-poms.

"Not yet, Delaney," Dawn said, pulling down my left arm.

"Um . . . Okay," Lucas said.

"Aren't you glad?" Dawn asked, lifting her head to look at him. He didn't seem all that excited, but then, I've never seen Lucas super excited. It's like he's always on a low setting.

"Yeah. Thanks, I guess," he said. "Excuse me. We're about to start and I need to find my opponent."

People were taking their seats in front of the chessboards,

their faces getting all serious, just like Lucas's. He was now sitting across from Fiona McCorkle, who's super smart and always wears her hair in a long, tight braid. I watched as they shook each other's hands.

"Where should we stand to do the cheering?" I asked Dawn.

She glanced around the room. "You know, there really isn't a spot where everyone can see and hear us," she said. "So why don't we start cheering for Lucas and Fiona and then move from table to table?"

"That's a *great* idea!" I said, raising my pom-poms in the air.

"No need to cheer for me, Delaney," Dawn said. "Come on. They're starting."

We stood in the aisle between the end of their table and the big window. There were already a couple of pieces in the middle of the game board, which made me feel like we were late. If only they had a starting pistol, like at cross-country.

Dawn nodded at me — her signal for me to start us off.

"*Go, Lucas. Go! Go, Lucas. Go!*" I chanted, Dawn joining in after a while.

Lucas looked over at us. "But I don't want to go yet. I want to take my time and figure out the next step carefully."

I paused for a moment, thinking up a new cheer. "*Take your time! Take your time!*"

Eventually Lucas slid a pawn to one of the middle squares.

Fiona seemed ready because she quickly moved a white piece shaped like a horse head.

"*Go, horsey, go!*"

"That's a knight," Fiona said. "Get it right."

"Hey, that rhymes! *That's a knight! Get it right!*" I chanted, swishing around the pom-poms. "Thanks, Fiona."

"We should do a more general chant," Dawn whispered in my ear. "The game goes too fast or slow for us to concentrate on individual moves."

"Right," I whispered back. Luckily I had come up with a good cheer while I was practicing in the living room. I stood at attention, just as we had learned to do in Cheer Squad, and started it off. "Ready? Okay! *C! H! E-S-S! Chess players are the best!*"

"That doesn't quite rhyme, you know," Dawn said.

I thought for a moment. "*C! H! E-S-S! Chess doesn't make a mess!*"

"*Shhhh!*" Fiona spun around in her seat so fast, her braid whirled around and whacked her on the collarbone. "Can you please be quiet?" The look on her face made me gulp.

"Excuse me."

I looked up and saw Mr. Langerham standing on the other side of me. "Hi there, Mr. Langerham." I waved a pom-pom at him.

"Hello, Delaney. Can you please explain what's going on here?"

Dawn stepped forward. "Yes, sir. I can. We are here on behalf of the JCMS Cheer Squad to boost morale."

I raised my pom-poms. "We're here to fire up the stands!"

"What stands?" Mr. Langerham asked.

"Right," I said. "I keep forgetting to check for those."

"We just want to spread spirit," Dawn explained. "You know, get everyone clapping and chanting and having a good time."

As she talked, Mr. Langerham started shaking his head over and over. "No, no," he said, "that's not going to work."

Mr. Langerham wasn't exactly mad, but he wasn't happy, either. He pointed out that he needed to maintain a low noise level. Together, the three of us decided that instead of chanting and yelling, Dawn and I would just whisper-cheer and shake our pom-poms anytime a chess team member made a move — a good one or a bad one, we could never tell the difference. It was much quieter, but also way more boring. But even though the pom-poms just made a swish noise, Lucas still said, "Can you please not do that? It's distracting."

"But how are we supposed to encourage you and boost your spirit if you won't let us, Lucas?" Dawn asked.

Lucas let out a long, loud sigh. "Tell you what. As soon as one of us wins, you can do all the cheering you want — *after* the game. Okay?"

"Deal."

So we stood and just watched. I wish I could say that I learned a lot and that it was interesting following the chess game. But it wasn't. In fact, after a while, I got tired of standing still. I had to resort to Wiggling Toes and Drumming Fingers (on my jeans instead of a desktop), plus a new coping technique I came up with called Bending Hips.

Just when I thought I couldn't take it anymore, Dawn elbowed me and waved a pom-pom at the board. Lucas was capturing Fiona's king. He had won!

"Hooray!" I cheered, jumping up and down. Only, on the up part of my jump, I accidentally hit a corner of the chessboard that was sticking out beyond the table a little bit. The next thing I knew, the board went flying. Chess pieces were flung up in the air and then started falling all around like rain. *Oops.*

Nobody clapped and cheered and had fun; instead they all stared at me with big frowns. I even heard a couple of cries of "Ow!" so I guess a few pieces landed on people's heads.

"Huh. Well, what do you know?" I said, trying to smile. "Chess really can make a mess."

CHAPTER EIGHTEEN

Dishonor

Dawn

It's not that we don't appreciate your commitment to cheer on the chess players and other students who normally don't get a lot of fanfare, it's just that . . . well . . ." Mr. Plunkett took off his glasses and squinted at me. "Your efforts don't seem to be helping."

Last period, Delaney and I both got official slips saying to go see Mr. Plunkett during our lunch break. I guess we should have anticipated what it would be about, but my first thought had been that we had gotten into Color Guard. Instead, here we were again, facing Mr. Plunkett, Coach Manbeck, and Mr. Langerham. It was the worst kind of déjà vu.

"Rather than boosting morale," Mr. Plunkett went on, "this experiment of yours seems to be creating bedlam."

"Delaney here just got carried away, is all," I said.

"I did. I'm sorry," Delaney said. "I didn't mean to flip over the board. I was just filled with the joy of triumph."

"The problem is that these people need to concentrate," Mr. Langerham said. "They are competing, and that takes focus."

"We know you had only the best intentions," Coach Manbeck said with a big, supportive smile. "Sports like football and basketball are inherently noisy, and cheering works in that environment. But when you bring loud cheers into other games, you end up being more of a distraction than a supporter."

I scowled. "So basically you're saying we shouldn't cheer at other competitions unless it's football or basketball," I said. "The way it's always been."

"Well . . ." Mr. Plunkett glanced around at the other adults. "Yes, I suppose that's what we're saying."

I tapped my finger against my chin, considering our options. I soon realized there weren't any. Still I sat there, feeling Delaney's eyes on me as she waited for me to speak on our behalf. I hoped a brilliant idea would pop into my head. But nothing did. Finally I said, "I believe we can abide by that."

"Good," Mr. Plunkett said. "I'm glad you understand." He looked up at Mr. Langerham and Coach Manbeck, standing on either side of him. "Is there anything else you all would like to add?"

They shook their heads.

"Thank you for coming. I'm glad we were able to resolve this," Mr. Plunkett said.

As everyone started heading out the door, Mr. Plunkett called to Delaney and me. "I want to remind you that my door is always open."

"Oh, okay," Delaney said. "We won't close it on the way out."

"No, I mean that you are always welcome to stop by and talk to me," Mr. Plunkett said. He put his glasses back on and smiled at us.

"Okay. Good-bye, Mr. Plunkett," Delaney said as she headed out.

"You know"—I paused in the doorway and glanced back at our counselor—"if we were in Color Guard, we probably would have been too busy to go to the chess match. Just saying."

He just smiled that barely-there smile at me and then turned toward his computer.

Darby was standing in the hallway waiting for us, her eyes wide and worried. "Are you guys in trouble?"

I let her stew for a while and walked a few yards away from Mr. Plunkett's open door toward the noise and bustle of the cafeteria. I hate to admit it, but I was still sore at Darby, and the fear in her eyes made me feel good. I waited several long seconds and then shook my head. "No, of course we aren't in trouble. We didn't do anything wrong. Delaney just got klutzy."

"But we agreed not to cheer anymore for competitions beyond football and basketball," Delaney added.

"Really?" Darby looked at me. "I'm sorry, Dawn. This was your big plan, and it must have been hard for you to give it up."

"Yeah, well, if you had been there, things would have gone differently," I said. "It would have been a stronger showing of support, for one thing. Plus, maybe you could have anticipated Delaney's mishap before it happened."

Darby hung her head. "I'm real sorry I let you guys down."

"It's okay, isn't it, Dawn?" Delaney said. "Darby's apologized, like, sixty-two times already."

"I'm real sorry I missed it," Darby said.

"Sixty-three!" Delaney said.

Darby walked over to me and looked me right in the eye. "We're still all for one and one for all. I promise."

Of all us triplets, Darby's probably the gentlest and the sweetest, so it's tough to stay cross with her. But I wasn't just angry. There were other things I was feeling — things I didn't tell my sisters. For example, I didn't tell them that I was scared. When the three of us aren't all united on something, it feels wrong and I don't know what to do. I couldn't fire Darby. But even if I could, who would I put in her place? It wasn't like I could go out and find another sister.

Nope. I had to be magnanimous and mature and forgive her — even if I didn't want to and she didn't deserve it.

"It's okay," I said, patting her shoulder. "I know you didn't mean to betray us."

Darby blew out her breath. "Thanks," she said, smiling.

"Alrighty," I said, "let's put this behind us and take a solemn pledge." I held my hand out flat in the air, waiting for them to add their left ones; then I would put on my right one, followed by their right ones, thereby making a tower of hands. It's our most weighty and dignified oath.

Only neither of them put their hand on top of mine. They just stood there, Darby with her bowed head and Delaney glancing all around while hopping on her toes.

"What's wrong?" I asked.

"I just . . . I mean . . . do we have to do it here?" Darby asked.

"Yeah. There are so many people around," Delaney said. "And I've suffered enough humiliation these past couple of days."

"But . . . it's our solemn oath." It was kind of an obvious thing to say, but it was all I could think of at the time.

"Couldn't we just do the pledge with words?" Darby asked, lifting one shoulder in that shy way of hers.

"Yeah, that should work," Delaney said. "It would still be binding without the hand stuff. Right, Dawn?"

Suddenly I realized what was going on. They were all embarrassed about being seen. It was worse than insubordination — they were ashamed of our proud Brewster triplet tradition. I felt a stinging sensation and my eyes filled with tears.

I hate it when I cry. It ruins everything — my voice, my vision, my thoughts. If I had my way, I'd never cry. Ever.

"Forget it," I said, sounding a little hoarse. "No need to pledge. Let's just get to class."

I turned and headed in the direction of my fourth period before they could notice my tears. On the way, I went into the bathroom and hid in a stall until I calmed down.

Things were so different lately. The kind of different that means bad things are going to happen — like the low, ominous music that starts playing in a movie before the monster jumps out. I recognized these not-right feelings. I felt them a long time ago, right before Dad moved out.

Nothing really bad was happening . . . yet. But it could. Maybe it had already started.

I'd said it wasn't a big deal that my sisters didn't want to do the oath, but it was. And that was another terrible sign: I'd lied to my sisters.

CHAPTER NINETEEN

Double Jeopardy

Darby

The next day in Mrs. Champion's class I let my guard down. I'd been trying to concentrate on the discussion, listening for when I needed to hide, but then I saw that colorful map of the United States on the wall and started daydreaming. I looked at the big peach-colored shape of Alaska and thought it looked like the profile of a bearded man — like Santa Claus without his hat. Then I heard someone call my name.

"Darby? Darby Brewster?"

It was Mrs. Champion. She was leaning against her desk and looking right at me. So was everyone else.

I gulped so loud, I bet people in Alaska could hear it.

Why didn't I listen more closely? This was what I got for being so daydreamy. I could have bent over to tie my shoe while she was looking for someone to call on. Or, like last Tuesday, I could have asked to go to the bathroom when it seemed like she was ready to move on to someone else.

But I didn't do any of those things. And now everyone was waiting for my answer. Only I couldn't talk — all I could do was sit there and swallow.

"Darby?" Mrs. Champion said again. "We were talking about how the people of the Indigenous Nations in what became Texas started making stone tools around 1500 BC. Can you talk about how technology has changed your life in some way?"

This time I opened my mouth to reply, but all that came out was a high-pitched noise. I sounded like those squeaky toys Quincy likes to play with.

"Mrs. Champion?" Wanda was waving her arm.

"Yes, Wanda?"

"Darby lost her voice."

Mrs. Champion frowned. "She did?"

"Yep. She's not sick anymore or anything, she just can't talk. It comes out all squeaky, like you heard."

"Oh. I see." Mrs. Champion looked at me again, her head tilted sideways as if I were a painting in a museum. "Is this an aftereffect of your sickness last week?"

I nodded. I figured it wasn't too much of a lie since the two incidents actually were kind of related.

"All right, let's move on." Mrs. Champion called on Elroy Littlefield instead. Elroy started talking about how a new app on his phone lets him take care of a cartoon dog named Peewee and so he's learning to be more responsible. I couldn't imagine that taking care of a cartoon dog would be anything like taking care of a real live dog like Quincy. But of course I didn't say anything.

When everyone seemed to be listening to Elroy, I wrote *Thank You* on the margin of my paper and turned it so that Wanda could see it. She put her hands in her lap and made them into thumbs-up.

It felt good to have a friend who was looking out for me — just like my sisters do. At the same time, though, I felt ashamed about all the lying. Dawn says that politicians have to twist the truth a little sometimes when they are trying to get elected, but I don't think Supreme Court justices do that. They're all about doing what's right. I bet Ruth Bader Ginsburg never told a fib to her teacher.

When the bell rang, I jumped up and started to follow Wanda out of the room, but Mrs. Champion waved to me.

"Darby, can I talk with you for a moment?" she said.

A cold, tingly feeling swept over my face, as if I were suddenly in Alaska. In winter.

"It's all right," Mrs. Champion said. "I'll do all the talking."

I stood silently beside her and waited as all of the students filed out of the room. She then shut the door and turned toward me.

"I'm sorry to hear you lost your voice," she said. "You've had a lot of bad luck lately and haven't been able to participate in our discussions."

I didn't know what to say to that. And anyway, I supposedly had no voice, so I just shrugged.

"I have to remind you that progress reports go out in two weeks. If you don't speak up in class by then, you'll have a zero for participation. That will bring down your grade considerably, and a note will be mailed home informing your parents."

My shame felt extra heavy, as if I were wearing a big metal coat. I couldn't lift my head and look her in the eyes.

"Do you understand, Darby?"

I nodded, still focusing on the carpet.

"All right then. You're excused. I hope you feel better soon."

Mustering up my energy, I made myself look at her and smile a little. Then I quickly turned and sped out the door.

Wanda was waiting for me in the hall.

"Are you in trouble?" she asked. Behind her bangs, her eyes were big and worried.

"Not yet," I said. "But I will be soon if I don't figure something out. I . . . I . . ." I swallowed hard and made myself say the rest of the sentence. "I'm probably going to get a bad grade."

"Oh no! Just because you won't talk?"

I nodded.

"That class is all wrong for you," she said, shaking her head. "Could you maybe get a different one?"

A thought popped into my mind so fast and so big, I

stopped walking. Wanda had to double back to where I was standing.

"You know . . ." I said, "there might be someone I can talk to about this."

"Really? Who?"

There were only a few minutes left before I had to get to my next class. I didn't have time to explain. "I'll tell you later, okay? Thanks again for your help. Bye!"

Quickly as I could without getting in trouble for running, I trotted around a corner and headed down the corridor where the administrative offices were.

Mr. Plunkett's door was wide open, just as he says it always is.

"Excuse me, Mr. Plunkett?" I said, poking just my head inside his office.

He looked up at me and took off his glasses. "Yes, Dawn?"

"It's Darby, actually."

"I'm sorry. Please come in, Darby. How can I help you?"

"Well . . . it's not for me, really. I'm asking for a friend." Another lie. But I figured I had already told so many on this topic, maybe one more little one wouldn't matter as much.

"I see. Go on." He motioned toward a chair and I sat down.

"So my friend, she's in this class and it's not going really well," I said, staring at the spot where the leg of his desk mashed down into the carpet. It was easier to not tell the truth when I wasn't looking at him. "In fact . . . my friend . . . she might not make a good grade."

144

"And your friend — she usually does well in class?"

"Oh yes. She always does. But this teacher has a different way of doing things, and it's really hard for her. Should I — I mean, should she ask for a schedule change?"

"Hmm." Mr. Plunkett grabbed a tissue from a box on his desk and started cleaning his glasses. "Let me ask this. Are there any things that your friend likes about the class?"

I thought for a moment. Wanda was in the class; that was the best thing. But also, I liked that Mrs. Champion tied history to our everyday lives, showing how it affects us even if it happened a long time ago. The discussions were interesting — even if I found it difficult to take part in them. Plus, she had cool posters on her walls.

"Yes. Lots of things, actually."

"Well, Darby, I would tell your friend that she should figure out another solution to her problem. Changing classes should be a last resort. And, as you and your sisters already know, it isn't always an easy thing to do."

I nodded slowly. He was right. Maybe there were other options I could try first, before asking for a change.

"And if she wants, your friend should come in to talk to me about it," he added. "I'm glad she has someone like you looking out for her."

My throat felt tight. Before I realized what I was doing, I said, "Mr. Plunkett? I'm the friend. It's me."

"You're the one having problems in a class?"

"Yeah." I stared down at my lap. "I'm sorry I lied to you."

"I appreciate your telling me the truth now. Why do you think you lied?"

I thought for a moment. "Because I was ashamed."

"About not doing well in a class?"

I nodded.

"Darby, lots and lots of students end up not doing well in a class — for all kinds of reasons. That's nothing to be ashamed about."

"But also . . . we're sort of used to solving problems on our own."

"You and your sisters?"

I nodded again.

"There's no shame in admitting a problem and asking for help. It's why I'm here. To help people."

I just kept on nodding. I was starting to feel like a bobble-head doll.

"Have you confided all this to your sisters yet?"

"No," I said.

"Why not?"

I shrugged. "We've been focused on other things. And I only just found out about my grade a few minutes ago."

"Well, I hope you find a way to work it out. Just remember, if you can't solve things yourself, it's okay to ask for help. Everyone has problems now and then."

"Thanks, Mr. Plunkett." And I grinned so big, I bet people in Alaska could see it.

CHAPTER TWENTY

Adjournment

Delaney

I'd just hopped off the final step of the stairs and was heading down the hallway to the living room when I noticed movement out of the corner of my eye. Lily was in her room, twirling and muttering to herself.

This was strange because normally I'm the one who twirls — not Lily. Wondering what was going on, I forgot where I was going and why, and stood in her doorway. That's when I noticed something else strange: On Lily's bed lay a suitcase, wide open like a yawning mouth.

"I'm going to be so late!" Lily said as she kept walking around her room, rummaging through things and peeking under furniture. "Where on earth did I put my blow dryer?"

"I know! I know!" I said, hopping up and down with my hand in the air. "I saw it in Mom's bathroom earlier. Hang on. I'll go check!" I was so happy to be able to help that I skipped all the way to the bathroom and back. "Here you go," I said, holding out her small blue dryer.

Lily looked relieved. "Oh, thank you!" she said as she wrapped the cord around the dryer and tucked it into her suitcase. "Wow. That was brave of you. I know you and Dawn are scared of that bathroom."

I blinked my eyes wide. "Right. The ghost."

I used to not even want to go near that room. All the weird groaning sounds scared me, and Dawn, Darby, and I were convinced that a ghost lived in there. Darby wasn't frightened. In fact, she thought it was neat and wanted to try and meet it. But Dawn and I felt we should stay far away. Only I hadn't thought about the bathroom ghost in months and months. In fact, I couldn't remember the last time I'd been afraid to go in there.

"That's so strange," I said, plopping down on Lily's bed, next to the suitcase.

"You okay, Delaney?"

"Yeah," I said. "But . . . I just realized I forgot about the ghost. I wasn't scared at all just now — not even a little bit. What do you think happened? Why am I not freaked out by it anymore?"

"You're growing up," Lily said as she put a few pieces of jewelry into a small leather case. "That's kind of how it works. You just wake up one day and realize you're different."

She'd said *different* like it was a happy thing and I should be proud. But I wasn't. To me, it felt like the wonky kind of different. Not bad or good, just weird. Like when Mom rearranges the living room furniture during one of our weekends with Dad. Or when my second-grade teacher got a haircut and looked like a whole new person. Or when I go to a Cheesy Weezy's in another town and the counter is on the left instead of the right — and they don't put as many pickle slices on their barbecue burger. The kind of different I'm not prepared for.

As I sat on Lily's bed, still reeling a little from the *different*, I stared at the open suitcase and the engagement ring on her finger. And it made me realize that there were lots more *different*s to come.

"Why are you packing?" I asked.

"I got some time off, so I'm heading out of town for a few days. I'm going to meet Clare in New Orleans."

"That sounds like fun." Clare was Lily's best friend all through middle school and high school. Clare went to a different college, though, and even studied overseas for a while, so now that they've graduated, they're trying to spend time together.

"I like Clare," I said, hopping off the bed and making faces at myself in Lily's dresser mirror. "I really hope you make her your maid of honor at your wedding."

Lily smiled at my reflection from behind me. "I'm sure she'll play an important part."

A pretty blue scarf was hanging from the edge of the mirror. I pulled it down and held it up, staring at the room through the gauzy material. It made everything seem foggy and distant.

A thought popped into my head, and before I realized it, I said, "Lily? Are you upset with me, Dawn, and Darby?"

She paused and looked at me. I turned around so that she'd be seeing the real me, instead of the Delaney in the mirror. "No. Why do you think so?"

"I don't mean that you don't like us or anything. I just mean . . . do you not trust us?"

"Of course I do! Why would you wonder about such a thing?"

I started twisting the scarf in my hands. "It's just that . . . you're getting married again and, well, we're worried that you're unsure about us because we kind of loused up your last wedding. We only did that because we love you and we love Alex and we didn't love Burton — not that we hated Burton or anything, it's just that —"

"Delaney." Lily had stopped packing and put her hands on my shoulders. At some point in my talking, I realized she was saying my name. "Delaney? Delaney, listen."

"Yeah?"

Lily stooped slightly so she was looking me right in the eye. "I'm not upset with the three of you for what happened last summer. Not at all. That wedding was loused up from the beginning. It was *my* mistake — not yours. And besides, everything has worked out for the best, right?"

"Well . . . yes." I glanced down at my hands. The scarf was now coiled up like a snake. I tossed it back onto the dresser. "But if you aren't upset with us, why won't you let us help you and Alex plan your wedding?"

"That's what you guys have been thinking?" She sat down on the bed and gave me a sad-looking smile. I nodded, and for some reason, my eyes filled with tears. Lily reached out and drew me into a big hug. "It's not true," she said into my ear. "I do trust you all. So much."

"You do?"

Lily let go and held me at arm's length. "Of course I do." Her eyes looked past me at her old-timey-looking alarm clock on her nightstand. "Oh, jeez," she said, standing, "I need to leave in five minutes. I'm so sorry, but I really do need to go. When I get back from my trip, I promise we'll all sit down and discuss this, okay?"

"Yay!" I said, twirling around and around. Lily wasn't upset with us! She didn't blame us for the Almost-Wedding Disaster!

Maybe we'd get to help with the wedding after all.

CHAPTER TWENTY-ONE

Party Loyalty

Dawn

I sat on the sofa, sighing and growling. I don't know where things went wrong, but ever since school started, mutiny has been afoot. My sisters don't seem as interested in doing things together. They're ashamed to take our solemn oath in front of people. And Darby even missed an important event. Now here I was, sprawled on the couch in the living room, waiting for Delaney to come play Parcheesi with me. Twenty minutes ago she ran upstairs to put on her lucky Parcheesi shirt, but she still hasn't come back. So either there's dissension in the ranks or she's just being plain inconsiderate.

I could ask Darby to play, but she's been in a real funk the last couple of days, sighing and staring off into space. While she normally stares off into space, this didn't seem to be her usual daydreaminess. Her shoulders were too slumpy and her expression too frowny.

I could ask Mom to play, but she's in the kitchen starting dinner, and even if she did agree to a game, she would probably give me an extra chore.

I could ask Lily, but lately she's been either coming or going and never seems to have time to just hang out.

I stood up, having just made up my mind to go on a search for a willing Parcheesi opponent, when there came a commotion down the hallway and Lily walked past, pulling a suitcase toward the front door. Behind her danced Delaney, saying, "Bye! Have a good trip! Bye, Lily! Bye!" Behind her came Mom and Darby.

I followed them out onto the porch and joined them in calling out "Bye!" Lily threw us a kiss before she climbed into her car and shut the door. We stood and waved as she drove off.

"Where's Lily going?" I asked after her Honda disappeared into the distance.

"No idea," said Darby with a shrug. "I just followed everyone."

"She's going to New Orleans to visit Clare," Mom said. "Good for her."

"And guess what?" Delaney pivoted as she bounced up and down, glancing from me to Darby. "I was just talking to her and she said she isn't mad at us. Maybe we can help her plan her wedding after all!"

"She said she isn't mad at us?" I asked.

"Yeah, I asked her if she was and she said no."

"Delaney!" I whacked my hand against my forehead. "Of course she's going to say no. She's Lily. She never wants people to feel bad."

Delaney gradually stopped bouncing until she was simply standing there, all hunched and wilted-looking. "Oh," she said, "I hadn't thought of that."

"Girls, is this about the wedding again?" Mom asked.

"Yep," said Darby. "Lily doesn't seem to trust us after her last one."

"I wish there was something we could do," I said, pacing around the porch. "Something that would show her we can be relied upon."

"You know what?" Mom's mouth slowly curved up into a grin. "I think maybe there is something you all could do for her. Something important."

"A tradition?" I asked.

"Yes, in fact."

"What is it?" Delaney restarted her hop. "What is it? What is it?"

We stood in a semicircle in front of Mom, leaning toward her eagerly. Mom put one hand on my shoulder and the other on Darby's. "How would you girls like to throw Lily and Alex a wedding shower?"

"Yes!" the three of us shouted, jumping up and down. It was a brilliant idea — so brilliant, I wish I'd thought of it myself.

"We could do that!" Darby said.

"We could definitely do that," Delaney echoed.

"And here's the best part," I said. "If we do a good job with the shower, maybe they'll let us help with the wedding!"

"I call this meeting to order," I said, pounding my fist on the back of the porch swing, making it jostle. "This evening we convene to discuss a historic event: the wedding shower of our sister, the amazing Lily Brewster."

"We get to be Shower Girls!" Delaney shouted, kicking her feet out.

"First item of business, planning the festivities. Do any of you have ideas?"

Delaney held up her hand. "I think it should be a surprise shower. You know. Where we tell all the guests about it, but ask them to keep it a secret. Then on the special day, Alex and Lily will walk into the house and . . . *ta-da!*" Delaney took a little hop into the center of the porch and opened her arms wide.

"I second that idea," Darby said, writing furiously in her notebook.

"And I vote yes, too," I said. "Great. Motion passes."

"Yay! We're *Surprise* Shower Girls!" Delaney said with a celebratory dance.

"You know," Darby said, "if this shower is going to be a surprise, we probably need to come up with a code word for it."

"How about *bath*?" Delaney suggested.

"Hmm . . ." I tapped my finger against my chin. "Don't you think that's kind of obvious?"

"Oh. Yeah," Delaney said. "Then how about cauliflower? It rhymes with shower."

"That'll work." Again, motion passed, and Darby wrote Operation Cauliflower in the minutes. Two motions down already! We had our mojo back. I felt better than I had in days. "All right, so what are we going to do for the party?" I asked.

For a long while, no one said anything.

"Come on." I pounded my fist on the swing again. "Let's hear some ideas."

Delaney shrugged. "I don't know what to do," she said.

"Yeah. What exactly happens at a shower?" Darby asked.

The three of us looked at one another, each of us shaking her head. There went our mojo.

"Well, that's just dandy," I said. "What now?"

"Can't we ask Mom?" Delaney asked.

"Not now, she's busy with dinner. Besides, this is our thing. We shouldn't bother her if we can help it."

"Hey, look. There's Ms. Woolcott. Maybe we should ask her." Delaney pointed to our next-door neighbor, who was weeding her flower beds and singing in a high, quivery voice like an opera singer. She was wearing a dress with big flowers all over it and a floppy, wide-brimmed hat. I was impressed at the sight of it. Ms. Woolcott's hair is so poufed up, I would never have thought a hat could stay on.

"Okay, let's do that," I said, both because I thought Delaney's idea had merit and also because I wanted to see the hat up close.

"Hi, Ms. Woolcott," we called out as we stepped down from the porch and crossed the yard to the fence.

"Why, hello, girls." She lifted the front brim of her hat to watch us. "What are you three up to?"

"We're planning a surprise wedding shower for Lily and Alex."

Ms. Woolcott gasped so loud, I was at first worried that a bee had stung her. "OH, my GOODNESS! That's the BEST news! They are SUCH a lovely couple. Ab-so-LUTE-ly perfect for each other!"

The three of us took a small step back. Ms. Woolcott doesn't so much talk as sing, and when she's excited, it's like listening to a turbo-powered mockingbird.

"So, um, Ms. Woolcott," I said, once she seemed to be finished, "we were wondering. You've been to wedding showers before, right?"

"Indeed I have."

"What sorts of things do people do there?" Delaney asked.

"Well . . ." Ms. Woolcott frowned in concentration, her eyes swiveling upward, as if there was a wedding shower going on in the sky. "Let's see, the guests eat nice finger foods. Like watercress sandwiches . . ."

"What's a watercress?" Delaney whispered in my ear. I shrugged.

"And they play games."

"Like Spite and Malice?" I asked.

"Musical Chairs?" Delaney asked.

"Presidential Trivia?" Darby asked.

Ms. Woolcott shook her head. "No, dear. *Bridal*-themed games. Like . . . Pocketbook Scavenger Hunt. That's when you have a list of items and all the ladies try to find them in their purse. Like mouth mints, a coin from the year you were born, red lipstick. It's de-LIGHT-ful!"

"But Alex doesn't carry a purse," I said. "Neither does Dad. Or Aunt Jane, come to think of it."

"Oh." Ms. Woolcott seemed taken aback. "Well, I'm used to showers that are just for the bride and her girlfriends. But these days there are all kinds of different rules. You should just plan something they would like. What do they enjoy?"

"Let's see . . . they like flowers," I said. "Real ones."

"That's good."

"And animals," Delaney said. "Oh! I know! Let's get a petting zoo!"

Ms. Woolcott's smile drooped. "Well, that's not typical. But again, it's for them. So maybe —"

"I think they'd enjoy a zip line!" Darby said.

I shook my head at her. "Darby. Don't even start with your reckless shenanigans."

"Whatever you three put together will be lovely, I'm sure," Ms. Woolcott said. "Now, if you'll excuse me, I see it's time for me to go feed Elvis." She motioned toward her house, where her big spoiled cat was frowning out the dining room window at us. "Please do stop by if there's anything I can do to help. Otherwise, I look forward to getting the invitation!"

She walked away, basket of flowers in one hand and garden shears in the other, singing the wedding march as she went. "Ya DUM da dum. Ya DUM da dum. Ya da da DEE da, da ya DUM da dum!"

"Huh," Delaney said after Ms. Woolcott went inside her house. "I guess that means she's coming."

"Well, it would have been rude to tell her about it, ask her advice, and then not include her," Darby said.

"I still think we should get some more ideas," I said. "Take some time to brainstorm and then report back. Remember, troops — Operation Cauliflower needs to be a success, no matter what."

CHAPTER TWENTY-TWO

Awakening

Darby

I was dreaming about clouds — big fluffy white clouds that could walk and talk, and I stood below taking lots of pictures — when something pushed against my shoulder.

"Wake up," said a voice. The cloud shapes went *poof*! And when I opened my eyes, a Dawn shape was standing over me in the darkness. "Good. You're up. Get out of bed, we have important business to tend to."

"What? Now?" I glanced over at the clock. "It's after midnight, Dawn. What are you doing up? Did you have a bad dream?"

"Are you kidding? I haven't been to sleep yet. I've been working."

"Working?"

Dawn made a huffing sound. "Well, somebody has to keep our official business going. And the hullabaloo about the wedding shower took up the whole evening. As great as it is to do something for Lily and Alex, we can't lose sight of our original goals — our commitment to spread equality; our responsibility to right wrongs wherever we may find them. Now, can you please poke Delaney?"

At this point, I knew I had no other choice. Once Dawn gets to speechifying, there's just no stopping her.

I slid out of bed, tiptoed over to Delaney, and tapped her on the arm. "Delaney?"

"No cheese," she mumbled.

"What? Delaney, wake up." I bent down and shook her shoulder.

Delaney turned over so that she was facing away from me. "Why is he wearing a hat?" she asked, her eyes still closed.

Delaney talks a lot of nonsense while asleep. Dawn says it's because Delaney can't help babbling, even in her dreams. Sometimes it's annoying, but mostly it's kind of funny. I thought my cloud dream was pretty cool, but judging by what she says, Delaney must have amazing adventures as she slumbers.

As I continued to shake Delaney's shoulder and call to her, a big white cone appeared beside me. "Wake up!" Dawn said through the megaphone. And somehow, quick as can be, Delaney was on her feet.

"What's going on?" she said, blinking hard and wavering slightly.

Dawn set down the megaphone and sat cross-legged on her bed. "I call this meeting to order," she said, pounding the headboard.

"Now? Really? Am I still dreaming?" Delaney said.

"Nope," I said. I turned on the lamp next to my bed and found paper and a pen so I could take minutes.

"What's gotten into you, Dawn?" Delaney asked, rubbing her eyes.

"Look, this is important," Dawn said. "And it won't take long at all. I wouldn't have woken you up, but it's time sensitive."

"Time sensitive?"

"Yep, in that we need to take action tomorrow. I just got off the computer" — she pointed to the front of the room where the old laptop on our desk was still glowing — "and I'm happy to say that I've found us a new event to go cheer at for Operation Cheer-for-All."

"But . . . I thought we weren't going to do that anymore," Delaney said.

"I thought we *weren't allowed* to do that anymore," I said. "Didn't we promise not to?"

"People, people. How soon you forget." Dawn shook her head in that smug way she sometimes does. "We promised not to cheer for any more *competitions*. But this isn't a competition. It's a show."

I was almost afraid to ask. "Um . . . what kind of a show?"

"A goat show."

"Okay, I really am still dreaming, aren't I?" Delaney said, rubbing her eyes.

Dawn slid off her bed and faced us, arms crossed and legs apart — like a giant letter *A*. "Look, the 4-H Club will be proudly displaying show goats at the Ranch Park tomorrow after school. Anyway, they never get any attention from Cheer Squad, so we should go there and boost their spirit."

"The goats?" Delaney asked.

"The 4-H Club!" Dawn threw up her hands.

"And you're sure we won't get in more trouble?" I asked.

"Why would we?" Dawn said. "All we'd be doing is acknowledging their hard work. And what's wrong with that?"

For a moment, no one spoke. While I knew Dawn meant well, and technically we weren't going against the promises we made to Mr. Plunkett, I still felt uneasy. It wasn't just that I was afraid of getting another office slip, either. It was that, for the first time, I was getting tired of all the last-minute meetings and covert operations. Things were complicated enough without Dawn pushing her brilliant ideas on us.

But I didn't have the heart to say this. For some reason, it was just so important to Dawn that we do this. So I sat there like Petrified Darby and kept quiet, just like I do in history class — which was something else I hadn't spoken up about. Adding that to my thoughts made me feel even worse.

"Do I hear any further objections?" Dawn asked.

Again, we were silent.

"All those in favor?"

Delaney and I both voiced our feeble-sounding ayes.

"Okay then. Motion passes." Dawn pounded her head-board. "I guess if there's no other business, we should probably get back to sleep."

Delaney plunked over sideways like a felled tree.

After Dawn had woken me, I couldn't wait to be left alone so I could return to my cloudy dreams. But now that I was up, with bad thoughts tormenting me, I knew I couldn't go back to sleep until I'd done something about it.

I raised my hand, but then realized she probably couldn't see it in the dim light. "Dawn? I think I have something to say. Something I need to tell you guys."

"Some new business?" Dawn asked.

"Sort of. I . . . um . . . I'm failing history."

"You're *failing*?" Dawn's mouth dropped open.

Delaney sat up again. "*You're* failing *history*?"

I hung my head in disgrace.

"What happened?" Delaney asked.

I took a deep breath and explained about the way Mrs. Champion runs her class, and how she'd told me that if I didn't participate in the discussion soon, I'd get an official progress report about my bad grade.

"This might be an obvious question, but how come you don't just speak up?" Dawn asked.

I lifted my shoulder. "It's difficult. You know how I am."

"You've spoken up before," Delaney said. "You gave a speech at the Almost Wedding."

"That was different. I was surrounded by friends and family there. Here it's with a bunch of kids and a teacher I don't know very well."

"But how can you say you don't know anyone in your class? This is a small town. We knew a lot of them before we were potty trained," Delaney said.

I drooped even more. "I mean . . . I know who they are. I just don't know them like I know you guys, or Alex, or the Neighbors, or . . ."

"I get it," Dawn said. "So what are you afraid might happen if you try to speak up?"

"Let's see . . ." Delaney started counting on her fingers. "She could faint or throw up, or remember that time in third grade when she hid behind the big potted plant all day?"

It was nice that Delaney appeared to be on my side, but hearing her rattle off all those times I was shy made me feel even more ashamed.

"Hmm." Dawn tapped her chin with her finger. "I hate to say it, but you're right. This could get worse and end up being a far bigger problem. We have to do something — something drastic. And I think you two already know what that is."

CHAPTER TWENTY-THREE

By Proxy

Delaney

At school the next day, Darby and I wore the same shirt and the same type of jeans. The only thing different was our shoes and our hair clips. Dawn reviewed our grand plan as we stood in the foyer before the bell rang.

"All right then. Darby, you will be Delaney and go to her Spanish class in room . . . what is it again, Delaney?"

"Room 203."

"Right. And Delaney, today you'll go to Mrs. Champion's room and be Darby, and I'll be her the next day. Remember — participate in the discussion, but don't babble. Just talk a little and act shy, otherwise you might give yourself away."

"Got it," I said, hopping on the toes of my sneakers.

"Also don't hop like that."

"Right." I made my feet stop. It worked, but then the wiggles moved to my knees.

Being Darby is hardest for me. When I'm Dawn, I just

make my eyebrows frown a lot, like I'm thinking up strate-gies all the time. Plus, she does this thing where she taps her index finger against her chin.

But Darby is the quietest of the triplets — the one who can sit still and do nothing. And both of those things are difficult for me. So whenever I'm Darby, I try to put on a daydreamy expression and look a little bit timid. I also try to say the word *mirror* in a sentence because Darby pronounces it differently from Dawn or me. She makes it one syllable — *meer* — instead of two.

People might think that my sisters and I trade places a lot, but really we've only done this a few times in our whole triplet history. We can never fool our family or people really close to the family, like Alex, so that limits us. But mainly we don't try it more often because it's tough to pull off. So we have to have a really good reason for it — like today.

"Delaney, you're bouncing again," Dawn said.

"Sorry, I'm just nervous. Darby, what do you do when you're nervous?"

She looked up toward the ceiling for a moment, a sign that she's thinking hard. "I climb a tree," she said.

"I mean, what do you do at school?"

"Sometimes I bend down behind my desk so no one can see me."

"I can do that!"

"All right. Bending, no bouncing," Dawn said. "After class, you guys will meet in the girls' room by the library, and switch out your shoes and change hairstyles. Then you can be yourselves again."

"Thank you, Delaney." Darby put her hand on my arm and gave it a little squeeze. "And you, too, Dawn. I'm sorry I'm so shy."

Dawn shook her head. "I blame myself that we're in this situation. We should have started your speaking-to-strangers practice earlier in the summer. I failed you as a leader."

Just then the bell rang and students started scurrying everywhere. I automatically headed for the middle hallway, toward my Spanish class, and then heard Dawn shout something. That's when I realized I was going the wrong way. I quickly turned and zoomed the other direction, almost knocking down a couple of sixth graders. Out of the corner of my eye, I saw Dawn slap her hand to her brow and shake her head.

I needed to start acting more Darby-like. First off, even though it was hard, I made myself slow down. I knew most people didn't move as fast as I did. But how could they stand it? I felt like a snail on crutches.

After what felt like six months, I finally reached the classroom. Last night, Darby had drawn a map of the room and marked where her desk was. She's good at drawing, so I found it easily. She'd even sketched in a cartoon girl with dark hair hanging in her eyes.

Even after she'd told us about it and drawn the map, I was surprised to see the desks in an oval shape. It kind of made me want to turn a cartwheel in the middle, but I didn't. Because Darby wouldn't do that.

I counted the desks from the teacher's spot and noticed a girl whose hair was short in the back and long in front. I recognized her from the map and knew that the empty spot next to her was Darby's usual seat. The map also said the girl's name was Wanda.

"Hi," she said to me when I put down Darby's backpack and settled into the chair beside her.

"Hi," I said. "Wow. You look just like your picture."

She seemed really confused and that's when I realized my mistake. Also, I thought I recognized her from one of my other classes — only I wasn't sure which one.

Luckily, at that point the tardy bell rang and the teacher started calling out instructions. Everybody had to get their textbooks and read pages 33 to 35 until the morning announcements came on. Darby had already warned me about the flag being high on the wall behind her — she'd even drawn it carefully on the room map — so I was ready when it came time to do the Pledge of Allegiance.

Saying the Pledge with my sisters is one of the things I miss most about not being in class with them. It's the most dignified thing we do all day, and I loved hearing our voices blend together in unison. When we were all done and sitting back down, I noticed a few people staring at me. Then Mrs. Champion said, "My, Darby. That was well done. I'm glad your voice is feeling better."

I was so embarrassed that I had forgotten to say the Pledge like Darby that I blushed a little and ducked my head. Luckily, that's a very Darby-like thing to do, so I was pretty sure I fixed everything.

"All right, everyone, if you haven't yet finished the reading, you can do so tonight as part of your homework," Mrs. Champion said as she slowly paced around inside the oval. "Now let's begin our class discussion."

I noticed that the girl next to me with the great haircut was watching me. I wasn't sure what to do, so I just smiled and waved to her, only because I thought Darby might have done that.

"Turn to page thirty-seven," Mrs. Champion said. There was a lot of shuffling as all the students followed directions. When it got quiet again, she said, "Now, the Caddo Nation was one of several tribes organized into a confederacy." She held up the textbook and pointed to the graphic that illustrated how the society worked. On the screen behind her was a projection of the website for today's Caddo Nation. "By 'confederacy,' I mean that each tribe in this alliance kept its own unique characteristics, but they all worked together as a unit when it came to major decisions. Do you think this was a good arrangement? If so, why?"

A few students called out answers like "strength in numbers" and "I'll scratch your back, you scratch mine." I remembered this unit from my history class. Only my teacher didn't really have us talk about it. Mainly we did worksheets.

"Good answers," Mrs. Champion said. "Can any of you share a time when you worked together with people to solve a problem?"

I sat up super straight. This was my chance! Or Darby's chance, actually.

"Mrs. Champion?" I said, raising my hand.

"Yes, Darby. I'm so happy you'd like to contribute. Go right ahead."

I realized I wasn't sure if they stood up to share or not, but it seemed like the thing to do when speaking to a group. So I got out of my chair, opened my mouth, and then . . . I froze. Because I hadn't actually thought about what I would say. When had I (or Darby) worked with people to solve a problem? That was difficult. Not because we'd never done anything like that. It was tough because we did that all the time. When you're a triplet, you're always consulting with your sisters, coming up with plans, and figuring things out together.

Luckily, pausing like that made me seem shy, which is a very Darby way to be. Mrs. Champion walked a little closer and smiled at me. "It's all right, Darby. Say whatever it is you want to say. There's no right or wrong answer."

I nodded, took a deep breath, and shared the first thing to pop into my head.

"One time our mom was going to make a peach cobbler and she got out a big bag of flour from the pantry and set it on the floor. Then the phone rang and when she came back, she found that Quincy — our dog — had gotten into the bag and there was white all over the place. Like snow! It was kind of déjà vu because of what happened last Christmas — but that's another story. Anyway, Quincy looked like a ghost dog because he was covered in flour. We had to put him in his crate in the backyard so we could clean. Mom was so mad, every time she scooped up some flour with the dust-pan, she would go outside and dump it on his head. So then, once we got the kitchen clean, my sisters and I had to give Quincy a bath. But when we sprayed water on him, the flour got all sticky and he looked like a dog made out of clay. It took a lot of washings and rinsings, but finally we got him clean. And for dessert, Mom gave us peaches and ice cream — which is good, but not as good as cobbler." I paused for a second. "The end."

It was real quiet as I sat back down.

"Okay," Mrs. Champion said. "Thank you, Darby. Anyone else want to share?"

I clapped my hands together under the desk to give myself a high five (which I guess is actually a low five). It felt good to help out my sister.

Once Mrs. Champion had walked to the other end of the oval, the girl with the cool hair leaned sideways, toward me. "So where's Darby today?" she whispered.

"She's in Span —" I stopped whispering and my face went tingly. "I don't know what you mean."

The girl's eyebrows went up — at least I think they did because her bangs seemed to go even lower. "Why didn't she come today?" she went on. "Is it because she's too shy to talk?"

I glanced all around to make sure no one was listening or watching. Then I nodded.

Wanda shook her head. "Too bad. I brought something I wanted to give her."

"What is it?"

"No offense, but I don't want to say. I'd rather it be a surprise."

"You aren't going to tell Mrs. Champion that we did a switcheroo, are you?"

One side of her mouth smiled. "No," she said. "And you won't tell Darby I have something for her? So it can be a total surprise?"

"Sure thing." And we shook hands on it.

CHAPTER TWENTY-FOUR

Concession

Dawn

Everything had gone okay with Delaney posing as Darby. And we were all set to meet up at the 4-H Club show later. That left one thing on my to-do list for the day.

Mr. Plunkett was typing on his computer keyboard when I showed up at his office after school. In fact, he was typing so fast and loud, it took him a long time to notice me. Eventually he glanced up.

"Hello, Dawn. Come on in and sit down." He took his hands off of the keyboard and gestured toward one of the chairs across from him. "It is Dawn, right?" I nodded.

"I won't be long," I said, leaning against one of the chairs instead of sitting. "I have to be somewhere soon. I just came by to see if there have been any additional openings in Color Guard."

"I'm afraid not. I'm sorry." And he did look a little sorry.

"Could you just check anyway?" I smiled sweetly. "In case there were some changes, but you were so busy you forgot?"

"Sure. But I need a minute to finish this up. Have a seat while you wait."

I checked the clock on his wall. "I guess that would be all right," I said, plopping into the chair I'd been leaning on. Darby and Delaney and I didn't have to be at the goat show for a little while, and I'd already told them during Cheer Squad that I'd meet them there. I wanted to make sure Mr. Plunkett hadn't forgotten about us and our situation.

As he typed, I glanced around his office and spotted a couple of things I hadn't noticed before. Like a framed photo of a boy that looked like Mr. Plunkett if he had been shrunk down in size and splattered with freckles. I also noticed a small framed poster on the wall to the left. It showed a person in one of those big rubber unicorn-head masks who seemed to be dancing with maracas. Below in colorful text was the quote "Be yourself; everyone else is already taken." The last thing I noticed was a tall spiky plant in a green pot. The tips of the leaves were turning brown and seemed more raggedy than they should be. I felt sorry for it.

"This year hasn't started off the way you'd hoped, has it?"

"Huh?" I was so lost in thought, it took me a while to realize Mr. Plunkett had said something to me. "Oh. Yeah. I mean, no, it hasn't."

He spun around in his chair so that he was facing me

instead of the computer. "Well, I'm afraid there's still just one opening in Color Guard. Would you like me to transfer you into the class?"

I let out a long sigh, slowly slumping like a punctured balloon. "No. Thank you, though. We're all for one and one for all — so it has to be three openings."

Mr. Plunkett tilted his head as he looked at me. "Why is it so important for you three to remain together?"

"Because," I said with a shrug. "Because we've always done almost everything together. It's who we are."

"I see. But who are *you*? Do you know what *you* want?"

"Of course I do. I'm going to be president someday." I lifted my chin proudly.

"Do Darby and Delaney want to be president, too?"

I laughed at that. "No way. They aren't interested in the job. But they want me to have it."

"I see." He nodded slowly and tapped his fingertips together. "So you three do have some different interests."

"Well . . . yeah. But we're still a team," I said. "I'm going to be president, Darby is going to be chief justice of the Supreme Court, and Delaney is going to be Speaker of the House. It's like . . . baseball. Different positions, same team."

Mr. Plunkett smiled that little smile of his. "Good analogy," he said. "What if you were to end up separated? On different teams? What's the worst that could happen?"

"That's the craziest notion I ever heard," I said with a chuckle. "You clearly don't realize how much my sisters need me. Without me, they'd be like . . . ice cream without the cone. Pancakes without syrup. Chips without salsa." Since he liked analogies so much, I figured I'd keep using them. And obviously I was hungry.

"And you need your sisters, too?"

"Sure I do. Not all the time, though. Some days I need them a lot, and some days I need them a little. Some days not at all."

"What about today?"

"Today . . . remains to be seen." I frowned down at my lap. "They've been kind of unreliable lately."

"How so?"

"At meetings they show up late or leave early. Even when they're present, they seem distracted. And Darby completely forgot an important meet-up." The more I talked, the more I could feel hurt and anger bubble up inside me — as if I'd packed up all those bad feelings into a soda can and just now popped the lid. "Anyway, I really think this might be your fault. This whole separated schedule thing is messing up everyone."

Mr. Plunkett looked surprised. "Is that so? You think things would be better if you had classes together?"

"Yep. I mean, I'm all right. I'm mainly concerned for the well-being of my sisters."

"That's good of you."

"Yep. The thing is, you're robbing them of my guidance. They feel lost."

"Hmm." He nodded and leaned across his desk, resting his chin on his hand. "And what are you being robbed of?"

"Well . . . my guidance. It's what I do."

I could tell Mr. Plunkett still didn't get how it was for me and my sisters. Of course, no one did. The plain truth was that we weren't as effective when we weren't together — and I wasn't as effective, either. United, we were the Brewster Triplets. By myself, I was Just Dawn. And Just Dawn, brilliant leader that she was, didn't have the same power as Dawn with her sisters. I was a different me, a not-as-good me. But this was hard to explain to someone who wasn't one of us.

"I'm sorry to hear you feel this way," Mr. Plunkett said, and again, he did look a little sorry. It helped settle down those feelings slow-boiling inside me. "But I do appreciate your giving this a chance. Keep trying it for a couple more months and we can check in again near the end of the semester. Okay?"

"Okay. But, you know, getting into Color Guard would sure help in the meantime."

"I understand."

"Well, I should go meet my sisters," I said, standing. "I'll be back tomorrow to have you check the class again."

"There's no need. If Color Guard gets two more openings, I'll let you know. You can trust me." He smiled that itty-bitty smile again.

I thought for a moment. "Yeah, but you're pretty busy and might accidentally overlook something. If it's all the same to you, I'd rather come here in person."

"That's fine. But you might end up waiting, like today."

"That would be all right. We could chat some more. Not that I need counseling or anything — I'd just be making polite conversation."

Mr. Plunkett took off his glasses and grinned bigger than I'd ever seen him grin before. "I'd like that," he said.

CHAPTER TWENTY-FIVE

Deserter

Darby

Darby!" Someone was calling my name as I was leaving school. I glanced up and saw Wanda trotting fast down the hall toward me. "What are you up to right now?"

"I . . ." I had no idea how to explain about the goat show. "Nothing."

"Can I join you?"

"Um . . . Sure, I have some time."

We fell into step together and headed through the big front doors, down the steps, and onto the curving sidewalk in front of the middle school.

"I have something for you." Wanda reached into her bag and pulled out another bag — a smaller, cube-shaped one. "Look inside," she said.

I knew what it appeared to be, and sure enough, as I

unzipped the top and lifted back the flap, there was a camera. It looked very similar to hers.

"Wow," I said.

"It's my dad's old one," Wanda said. "He noticed I was getting into photography, so he gave this one to me when he bought himself a new one. He told me to use it as a backup camera. I thought you could borrow it and try taking pictures on your own. The ones you took on my main camera were cool."

"They were?"

Wanda nodded. "You're good at observing and looking beyond the obvious. Your photos were really — what's the word? — dreamy."

"Thanks, Wanda." A warm, sweet feeling oozed over me, like hot fudge. I never thought I'd find something else I liked doing and might even be good at. It was as if I'd discovered buried treasure.

"Go ahead," Wanda said. She lifted the camera out of the bag and put the strap around my neck. "Try it out!"

"Are you sure you want to loan this to me?"

"Of course!" Wanda chuckled. "I tried to give it to you in history class, but your sister went instead of you."

My cheeks burned. "Yeah. Sorry."

"But anyway, you have it now," Wanda said. "I was hoping we'd walk around town again and take some more pictures. That was fun. Do you have time, or do you already have plans?"

Something inside me clicked into place, and just like that, I made a decision. I didn't want to go cheer for goats. I wanted to boost my own spirit. And I could do that by hanging out for a while with my new friend. "Yeah, I have time. Let's go take pictures."

"Yay!"

We followed the sidewalk to the street and headed south, toward the middle part of town instead of north toward the Ranch Park. The wind was blowing and dry leaves skittered along the sidewalk in front of us, as if challenging us to a race.

I liked how Wanda and I could be together and not talk for a while. We just walked and watched and listened. Once again, I felt as if I was seeing my surroundings for the first time. And I ended up taking lots of pictures — of flowers, front porches crammed with potted plants, the giant metal horned toad on top of the garden store, a starburst-shaped crack in the cement, and pretty shadows on the sidewalk.

"You know," I said as we sat on a bench overlooking the courtyard square, "I've lived here my whole life, but I've never appreciated how pretty and interesting this town is until I started taking pictures of it."

"Yeah," Wanda said, aiming her camera up toward the courthouse. "That's one of the things I love about photography. You're in the middle of everything, but you aren't making things happen. You're just there, noticing."

"And then you capture it on film so other people can notice."

Wanda grinned. "You're good at it, you know. You really should join photography class. Our teacher is hoping to get a couple more people to join. What are your electives?"

"Spanish and, um, Cheer Squad."

"Oh yeah. I saw you and your sisters at the pep rally. Do you like cheering?"

I shrugged. The answer was no, but I didn't feel like explaining how the three of us were in there just so we'd have a class together, and how we'd originally planned to do Color Guard. Now that I stopped to think about it, I wasn't all that disappointed about Color Guard anymore. I liked it fine — but not the way I liked taking pictures.

"Well, maybe you can take photography next year," Wanda said. Her voice sounded like someone trying to be cheerful, but who didn't entirely feel that way.

I considered her suggestion. I only got two elective classes, and one had to be a foreign language. That left just one opening. Knowing my sisters, they'd probably want us to sign up for Color Guard again next year. I couldn't imagine Dawn or Delaney wanting to take photography. I might be able to in high school, when we have more electives, but that seemed so far away.

Just as I started to feel sad, I pushed the bad thoughts away. I didn't want to fret about what my sisters wanted or wonder if I'll ever get to learn photography or worry about letting Dawn down by not showing up for the 4-H Club event. I wanted to be here, on the courthouse grounds, watching squirrels and taking pictures with Wanda.

I wanted to be in the Now.

CHAPTER TWENTY-SIX

Enlistment

Delaney

Cheer class had been super fun! Only . . . that was kind of a bad thing. Because it was so spectacular, I ended up being insubordinate and going against the plan my sisters and I ratified the night before.

When the bell rang, Dawn took off to see Mr. Plunkett and I was in the middle of a long run of jumps and cartwheels. I was just about to catch up with Darby so we could head over to the goat show together when suddenly I realized I'd left my backpack on the bleachers. I ran back to get it and was about to leave again when I heard Cherry let out a squeal and say, "That's so cute!" while staring at something on Lynette's cell phone. The rest of the eighth-grade cheerleaders were also standing around looking and going *Aww*. So then I was really curious and ran back again to take a peek, and saw the most adorable puppy! That made me want to tell them all about Mynah, and since I didn't have a cell phone with photos on it, I did my best impression of her bouncing and wriggly nose. When we were done, I started to leave, remembered my backpack again, ran and got it, and then I couldn't find Darby anywhere.

I started to walk over to the Ranch Park when Lynette poked her head out of the gym and called out, "Where are you going, Delaney?"

"Um . . . to see goats?"

"But today is cheerleader tryouts!" Lynette said. "You need to stay." Cherry and a few of the others came up behind Lynette and started calling out things like, "Yeah, stay!" and "You're so good!" and "You're sure to get picked!"

I stood near the school's front door for what seemed like a long time, feeling like the rope in a tug-of-war. Go or stay? Goat show or tryouts? Sisters or cheerleader pals? I knew what I wanted to do — but I wasn't sure if I should.

"Will it take a long time?" I called back to the other girls.

"No!" Lynette said. "You just cheer, that's all."

"Oh, okay!" I decided I could maybe do both and told myself Dawn would understand. Even if I was a little late, it shouldn't matter. After all, Darby would be there with her. Now, looking back, I think maybe I was trying to fool myself. And either I'm really good at fooling or I'm easily fooled.

Tryouts weren't hard — just cheering by myself and with the group in front of Coach Manbeck and the head cheerleaders — but it took a lot longer than I'd thought. Once it was done and I looked at the clock on the wall, I knew there was no point in heading over to join Dawn and Darby. That's when I realized what I'd done and guilt took over. It was like my heart was all heavy and droopy and trying to drag me down low. I couldn't have turned another cartwheel if I tried.

There was nothing left to do but go home and face my sisters' wrath.

It felt a little weird walking by myself. Even if one of us is sick, there's still another of my sisters headed home with me each day. It gave me that odd feeling that I was forgetting something — even though I'd already gotten my backpack. Twice. I even hummed a song as I went, so it wouldn't seem so sad and lonely, and kept a lookout for anyone else I knew. Unfortunately, the only people I spotted were strangers or were headed other directions.

Our route home passes by our old elementary school. Mostly I don't think much about it as we go past — we're usually too busy talking or I'm thinking about what's for dinner. But since it was just me that day, I stopped and leaned against the playground fence.

Even though the school day had ended already and the students had left the building, there were still a few kids on the playground. One boy kept going on the whirl-around slide — a big slide with a tunnel that goes in two curves. When I first started at that school, I thought that slide looked enormous and scary. But now it seemed small. And the swings didn't seem high off the ground, like I remembered. In fact, the entire playground seemed to have shrunk. It

made me feel kind of forlorn, and all the guilt and sadness made me drag my feet the rest of the way home.

Mom was laughing when I walked into the living room.
The sound seemed strange to me, since I was in such a low-
down mood.

"Are Dawn and Darby here yet?" I asked.

That's when I noticed Mom was on the phone. "Not yet,"
she said, holding it away from her face. Then she moved the
phone back near her mouth and said, "What was that, Jane?"

I perked up suddenly. "Is that Aunt Jane? Can I talk to
her? Please can I just say hello?"

Mom frowned and shook her head, trying to keep listening to Aunt Jane. Eventually she saw my pleading eyes and
sighed. "Fine," she said. "Jane? Delaney is here and wants to
talk to you."

She held the phone out to me. I snatched it up with a vic-
torious bounce.

"Hi, Aunt Jane," I said. "How are you? How's the campground? How's Mrs. Kimbro? How's Mo?"

Aunt Jane laughed. "I'm fine, and everyone around here is
fine — including that old donkey. In fact Mo has a new pal."

"A new pal? Who?" I asked, feeling a little jealous.

"Mrs. Kimbro got a puppy named Chloe, and she and Mo
are already the best of friends."

"*Awww!*" My voice went up so high it made Mom wince.
She made the *hurry up* sign with her hand and went into the
kitchen.

"Plus, the new dock is almost finished," Aunt Jane went on. "As soon as it's done and we have some new boats, you girls will have to come visit to test things out."

"That would be stupendous! Maybe we could call up Robbie and his brothers and invite them, too!"

"Great idea."

"I miss you, Aunt Jane. And I miss Robbie and Mo and Mrs. Kimbro's homemade biscuits and the big trees and the fish and . . . and . . ."

"Hey, hey, hey. It's okay, Delaney," Aunt Jane said.

I hadn't even realized I was crying a little, but I was. My voice had gone all high and wobbly and a tear had run out of each of my eyes, creating matching streaks down my face.

"Sorry," I said. "I'm just tired, I think. Maybe I need to eat more protein."

"Is school going all right? Your mom said you three had some disappointing things happen."

"Yeah . . ." I let my voice peter out. I wondered if I should tell her about cheerleading and Dawn's crazy plan and how I missed my sisters during the day but sort of got tired of them when they were around. Only, I wasn't sure if I could put it into words. It didn't make sense, all the feelings inside me — my mind was like that whirl-around slide, only with lots more turns.

"Anything you want to tell me about?"

I pondered this. It occurred to me that I could tell her about doing cheer tryouts instead of meeting Dawn and

Darby. Maybe I'd feel better if I admitted it and got some advice. But it was such a long story and Mom had already come back into the room and was motioning for me to give her the phone. "No," I said. "Just . . . I miss you."

"Miss you, too, Delaney-doo."

I handed the phone to Mom and trudged upstairs to our room.

When I got there, I did something I don't usually do. I just sat. I plopped down in the desk chair and tried to make my brain settle down. As I did that, my eyes wandered all around the room until they landed on something hanging on the wall: a flag, given to us by three brothers we'd met on our camping trip last spring. Robbie, the middle brother, had been an especially good friend to me, and we still sometimes sent each other postcards. He'd made the flag himself, and it was beautiful. The design was of six hands all holding on to each other at the wrist, making a hexagon shape — a symbol for the three of us becoming friends with the three of them.

A friend. Could that be what I needed right now instead of a sister or even a beloved aunt? Maybe I'd feel better if I confided in Robbie. Seemed strange to admit, but I'd never really gone to anyone outside of family for help before. Maybe it was time to try.

I spun around and found some paper and a pen in the nearby desk drawers. Then I took a deep breath and tried to put all my worries into words:

Dear Robbie,

How are you? How are Nelson and Jay and your dad? We are doing okay. Seventh grade started and it's been ~~fine~~ ~~adequate~~ disappointing.

I'm going to tell you a secret because I have to tell someone or it will explode inside me and then — who knows? — maybe I'll get real sick or lose my ability to speak or something. I can't tell any adults, because they just won't understand. And I can't tell my sisters because they're part of my problem.

Okay. Here goes. The secret is this: I think I really like cheerleading.

Only the thing is, I'm not supposed to like it — because Dawn and Darby don't like it. And we're all for one and one for all.

Anyway, thanks for listening. Wait, that's not right. We aren't talking. Thanks for reading. Well ... that's not exactly right

either because you haven't read this yet.
So I guess thanks for being a friend — the
kind of friend I can write things to and
it will make me feel better.

Your pal,
Delaney

CHAPTER TWENTY-SEVEN

Insubordination

Dawn

It was thirty-five minutes after meet-up time, and I was still the only official JCMS Pom Squad rep at the goat show. It was becoming increasingly obvious that my sisters weren't just late — they weren't going to come at all.

I wondered if I should go ahead and cheer by myself. I'd already scouted a good location — an empty square at the end of a row of pens where two aisles intersected. There were even a few folding chairs where people could sit and watch if they wanted to.

"Here goes," I said to myself. I stood in the square, tightened my grip on the pom-poms, and started to bounce . . .

But then I couldn't do anything else. It just seemed preposterous. Two or more people could be a pep squad, but if it was just me cheering and leaping about, it would probably look like I was bonkers. Plus, I wasn't very good at the leaping-about part. And with so many people busy walking, brushing, or giving haircuts to their goats, I probably wouldn't attract much attention.

I sat on a folding chair near one of the pens and crossed my arms — partly as an angry gesture and partly to hug myself. What was wrong with everyone? First the other pep squad representatives didn't show at cross-country, leaving it up to me and my sisters. Then Darby up and forgets the chess meet. And now she and Delaney were both no-shows. It had been a long, gradual uprising. A passive, inconsiderate resistance.

I heard a bleating sound and glanced over to find two gold eyes looking back at me. They were sort of like a giant cat's eyes, only the dark slits in the center went the wrong way — side to side instead of up and down. The sight of them made me yelp and jump out of my seat.

It was a goat, of course. And according to the ribbon on his pen, he was an excellent one. I noticed another, older-looking goat in the pen with him, but he (or she) just lay in the pine shavings looking bored. Meanwhile, this goat kept staring at me and twitching his ears. I wondered if he had a name. I also wondered why he seemed so interested in me.

"Hi," I said.

The goat made a snuffling noise and bobbed his head as if nodding.

"Yeah, it's just me," I said, as if he'd asked me a question. "No sisters this time. I don't suppose you have any siblings? No? Well, good for you. You don't have to worry about being stood up by people who share your DNA."

He kept on peering at me. His eyes didn't seem scary anymore. And I noticed they had long, pretty lashes.

"Then again, I feel a little sorry for you," I said. I turned around and leaned back against the metal rails of the pen. "Because when it works right, having sisters is the best thing ever." Down the aisle in front of me, I could see two little girls walking together. One looked about seven and the other looked around four. They were holding hands as they strolled along, pointing and chatting about the different goats. Seeing them gave me a twinge — as if my heart was being pulled and twisted like Silly Putty.

I could hear more snuffling behind me and knew that my goat pal was still there, listening.

"Maybe you're right," I said, as if he'd given me some great goat advice. "Maybe I shouldn't do things for them anymore. This morning I fed Quincy so that Delaney had time to find her favorite tennis shoes. And tomorrow I'm supposed to pretend to be Darby and talk in her history class so she doesn't get a bad grade. If they can't even show up for this, then maybe I shouldn't show up for them. Delaney can do her own dang chores. And maybe Darby should fail her class if she can't pipe up."

All that angry ranting made me feel a little more powerful and a little less sorry for myself, but the minute I said the words, I also knew I didn't believe them. I couldn't go against my sisters or do anything that might hurt them — not even if they deserved it.

"The thing is," I said to the goat noises behind me, "I thought my sisters needed me. But I guess they don't. And not only does that make me sad, it also makes me scared. How can someone be a leader without followers?"

The whole time I talked, the sounds behind me grew louder. It made me glad to know that the goat was still listening — at least he hadn't given up on me. But then I felt a weird tugging sensation.

I turned around and found myself face-to-face with the goat, who was chewing on something stringy and silvery.

"Aw, man. You too, goat?" I asked.

I'd thought he was such a good listener, but instead, my new pal had been eating one of my pom-poms.

It was mutiny all around.

CHAPTER TWENTY-EIGHT

Conflict of Interest

Darby

I winced slightly as I walked through the front door. I'd pictured Dawn and Delaney standing just inside, waiting to yell at me, but as I stepped into the foyer, I could see Mom sitting in the living room, typing on her laptop. There was no sign of my sisters.

"Hi, Mom," I said. I put down my backpack and borrowed camera and settled into the striped armchair. "How are things around here?"

She chuckled. "They're good. How was your day?"

"Oh, you know, fine." I wanted to ask her if she knew anything about Dawn and Delaney and how their day went, but I was too nervous. So instead, I brought up a safer subject. "Have you heard anything from Lily?"

Mom shook her head. "I'm sure she's having a great time with Clare. They've hardly seen each other these past couple of years. I'm glad they're doing this."

197

"Me too," I said.

"You know," Mom said, sitting back and looking over at me, "with Lily moving out, one of you could take her room and another could stay in the attic. Then I could move my office so another of you could have that room."

"But . . . why?" I must have looked as confused as I felt, because when Mom glanced at me, she seemed taken aback.

"So you can all have your own rooms, of course," she said. "I figured since you have separate rooms at your dad's, you'll want them here, too."

"But then you'll have no place to work."

"I'm always out here anyway" — Mom gestured about the room — "or at the dinette. And there's room for my files in my bedroom."

I'd just assumed Dawn, Delaney, and I would keep on sharing the Triangular Office indefinitely. Besides, we hadn't yet separated at Dad's new house, since our rooms weren't done yet, so it all still seemed theoretical. Even though I was excited about my new bed, whenever I closed my eyes and tried to imagine having my own room, I couldn't do it.

"Well, thanks, but that would be . . . premature. And unnecessary."

"All right." Mom had a strange smile on her face. "You three can just let me know when you're ready."

I thought it was strange that she was so sure it was a matter of "when" and not "if," but I didn't get to ponder it long. Because right then, the front door banged open. Dawn trudged inside carrying one pom-pom and one plastic pom-pom handle.

I jumped off the chair and ran up to her. "Hey . . . so, um . . . how'd it go?" I asked.

Dawn looked at me but didn't say anything. Her mouth and both eyebrows were heavy horizontal lines.

I glanced behind her. "Where's Delaney?"

Dawn gave me the same severe look as before, with an added glare as she disappeared around the corner. Soon I heard her stomping up the stairs to our room.

"What's going on between you two?" Mom asked.

"It's complicated," I said. Because it was. So much so, I couldn't have explained it to her — or anyone. "I wonder where Delaney is," I said, both wanting to change the subject but also because I was puzzled. I'd figured she would have come in behind Dawn, or more likely, ahead of her.

"She's upstairs in your room," Mom said. "She came home a little while ago."

"Oh." A prickly sensation swept over me. *Uh-oh*. That probably meant Delaney hadn't met with Dawn at the goat show. Or she'd gone and left really early? Either way, it looked like we'd both let Dawn down.

"I . . . gotta go talk to them," I told Mom as I headed out of the room. If they were up there discussing and deciding things, I needed to be there.

I could hear Delaney all the way up the stairs to the Triangular Office.

"Sorry! Sorry! Sorry! Sorry!" she was saying to Dawn, bouncing on every first syllable.

For some reason, the sight made me angry. Dawn had been counting on her. But also, I had been counting on the fact that she'd be there with Dawn when I'd made my decision. "How could you not go?" I said to Delaney, my voice louder and grumblier than usual.

Delaney stopped bouncing and apologizing and swiveled toward me. "Something came up," she said. "And anyway, Dawn just told me you weren't there, either. How come you didn't go?"

"Something came up," I said, my anger transforming into guilt.

We stood there, staring at each other. Neither one of us wanted to ask what had come up — because if we did, we'd have to disclose our own whereabouts at that time.

It wasn't that I was ashamed of my new friendship with Wanda, it was that I didn't want to share her or photography with my sisters the way I had to share everything else. I liked having something — someone — that was just mine.

I suddenly had a thought, one that made me feel cold and goose bumpy. "Dawn, are you still going to stand in for me tomorrow in Mrs. Champion's class?"

"I can't believe you asked her that," Delaney said. "I can't believe you asked her a favor when you stood her up today. I'm disappointed in you, Darby."

"But you also stood her up."

"Yeah. Well, I'm disappointed in me, too!"

Delaney's words hung in the air like thunderclouds. We stayed like that for a moment — Delaney and I standing opposite, eyeing each other suspiciously, and Dawn sitting on her bed, staring vacantly in the distance. On the wall above, I caught sight of the flag Robbie had made us on the spring break camping trip. The carefully shaded design of hands holding on to each other and the words UNITED IN FRIENDSHIP AND FUN carefully lettered across the top. Only we weren't united in friendship and fun. We were divided in woe. We even had secrets we were keeping from one another.

Dawn got to her feet and fixed me with a blank expression. "Of course I'm still going to be you tomorrow," she said. "I keep my promises — unlike other people." With that, she walked past us and went downstairs. She didn't yell, she didn't stomp, she didn't even frown. She just moved through the rest of the evening like she'd gone down to 10 percent of herself.

Sullen, defeated Dawn was somehow worse than irate, shouting Dawn. It made me want to help her — to attack whatever had done this to her. But then I'd remember. It was me.

Same with Delaney. Usually at dinner she was hopping in her seat, chattering on and on about the events of the day. But tonight she sat silent. So many times I'd wished for Dawn to be not quite so temperamental and for Delaney to be still and quiet. Only now that they were behaving that way, I hated it.

Mom noticed, too. After attempts at conversation went nowhere over our chicken and rice dinner, she asked, "What's gotten into you three?"

When we mumbled we were just tired, she suggested we forgo watching any TV after homework and just go to bed. I think she was surprised — and maybe more worried — when none of us challenged her on that.

That night we continued to barely speak. Just the occasional "Excuse me" or "It's your turn to feed Quincy" or "That's my Gryffindor toothbrush — your Hufflepuff one is over there." Even as we lay in our beds after dark, we turned away from one another or hid under blankets.

That's when I realized I could see what Mom had been talking about. I didn't want it just yet, but I was starting to imagine a time when we would all want our own rooms. The thought made me feel even sadder.

CHAPTER TWENTY-NINE

Marching Orders

Delaney

The next day all three of us wore our Wonder Woman T-shirts, white shorts, and white sandals, with our hair up in ponytails. It was mainly for convenience's sake, so Dawn and Darby wouldn't have to trade clothes after first period. But I went along with it, too, because I thought it was a nice outfit — and because it was comforting to be dressed like them after all the disagreements we'd been having.

To those who barely knew us, we probably looked exactly alike this day. But to me, it was still super obvious how to tell who was who. Dawn had a slight scowl on her face and Darby looked like she wanted to dive behind the first big piece of furniture she saw and hide there until the cover of night. I couldn't see my own face, so I don't know what I looked like, but I'm convinced it didn't match either of them. So even though Dawn, Darby, and I were more alike than usual on the outside, we were the most different we'd ever been on the inside.

Our walk to school started out excruciatingly silent. To make up for it, I sang songs and chanted cheers the rest of the way — only that just made Dawn scowl more fiercely and Darby sigh. Finally we arrived, and when the bell rang for first period, we went our separate ways — with Dawn going to Darby's history class and Darby going to Dawn's science class. I thought it was nice of Dawn to keep her word to Darby even after our betrayal.

Unfortunately, the day got weirder. At lunch, Darby sat with Wanda, and Dawn plopped down beside Lucas. So I ate with Lynette, Cherry, and a couple of other cheerleaders. But here's the strangest part . . . not sitting with my sisters didn't feel as awful or bizarre as I'd thought it would. It was a little sad, because we were sore at one another, but otherwise it was okay. I even had a good time.

Of course, this meant Cheer Squad class would be the real test.

As soon as Darby came into the gym and sat in the bleachers, I decided I was done with our estrangement and sat down beside her.

"Hi," I said.

"Hi," she said.

Neither of us sounded huffy, but we didn't sound all that happy, either.

When Dawn came in, she spied the two of us and walked over.

"Hi," Darby said.

"Hi," I said.

"Hi," Dawn said.

That made three not-huffy, not-happy hi's. Things were looking up.

Dawn plopped down on the other side of Darby, and for a moment or two, we just sat.

Then Darby turned to Dawn and asked, "How'd it go in Mrs. Champion's class?"

"Fine," Dawn said. "Except you got detention."

Darby gasped. "Detention? But . . . why?"

"During discussion you said that the Texas Revolution was over slavery and Tucker Burnett said you didn't know what you were talking about, that those Texans were brave, blah blah blah." Dawn opened and closed her hand as if it were a talking mouth. "Then you said, 'I didn't say they weren't brave, just misguided and wrong.' Then Tucker said you didn't know anything, and that's when you called Tucker a weak-minded tragedy and got detention."

"But I didn't call him that," Darby said. "You did."

"Well . . . technically you did. Because I was you."

That was as far as they got, because the bell rang at that moment and Coach Manbeck stood and faced all of us in the stands. I was still reeling from the news that Darby had detention, and I couldn't decide whether or not she should be mad at Dawn, since Dawn had been doing her a favor.

"I have some announcements," Coach said, raising her hands to help get everyone's attention. "I want to thank everyone who tried out for cheerleader after school yesterday. We had a lot of great candidates, and I want to emphasize that those of you who didn't make cheerleader will still be part of the Poms and an important part of this organization."

Oh yeah. Tryouts! With all the stress at home with my sisters, I'd almost forgotten.

"So now, without further delay, I will announce your new cheerleaders," Coach said. "Please come down as I call your name. Congratulations to . . . Crystal Chang, Bethanne Holbrook, Emmy Washington, and Delaney Brewster!"

Inside me, I felt a big burst of excitement, nervousness, and surprise. It pulled me up from my seat and rocketed me down the bleachers to stand beside Coach Manbeck and the other new squad leaders. Meanwhile, back in the stands, I could see my sisters stop their polite clapping and turn to look at each other. For the first time all day, their expressions matched — kind of wide-eyed and openmouthed. I caught their gazes, smiled sheepishly, and waved.

I knew I had a lot of explaining to do as soon as I sat back down, and I was already trying to come up with words in my mind. Words like "Oh yeah, didn't I mention it?" or "I was going to tell you but . . ." or "It completely slipped my mind."

Only I never had to use any of them. Because just then Lucas Westbrook, wearing his navy blue office-aide badge, walked into the gym and handed Coach Manbeck a slip of paper.

"Dawn? Darby? Delaney?" Coach said. "Mr. Plunkett needs to see the three of you in his office right away."

CHAPTER THIRTY

Truth to Power

Dawn

As usual, Mr. Plunkett was busy typing when we got to his office, so we just sat in the chairs and waited. I felt jumpy for some reason, as if any minute, a net would fall on top of us or our chairs would fall through a trapdoor. The leaves of his plant looked even browner and more jagged, so I took that as a bad sign. It had already been a rotten day, and I was braced for more lousy things to happen.

Eventually he took his hands off the keyboard and turned to face us. "Hello, girls. I bet you three can guess why I've called you in," he said, taking off his glasses.

"I can't believe this. We're summoned for wrongdoing again? All because of one unfortunate interaction with a goat?" I said. "Well, I want to go on record as saying that no competitions were thwarted and no animals were harmed due to our spirit boosting — which was just me, anyway, since my sisters turned on me." I paused to give emphasis to their treachery. "And besides," I said, "the goat ate my pom-pom, so if anything, he did the thwarting."

Mr. Plunkett just looked at me. Then he rubbed his eyes and put his glasses back on. "Uh, that's actually not why I called you in," he said.

"Oh. Never mind then."

"What's up, Mr. Plunkett?" Delaney asked.

"I'm happy to report that two more students are dropping out of Color Guard, and I can now add all three of you to the class." He sat back in his chair with a grin.

I stared at him, letting the words sink in. It seemed almost too good to be true. We could be in Color Guard together. We could get out of Cheer Squad. We could practice at home every day like we did over the summer and be the best in the school. Things could be better now!

Only, before I could say anything, Delaney raised her hand and waved it around.

"Delaney?" Mr. Plunkett said. "Do you have something to say?"

"Yes, in fact I have a bit of an announcement. And that is" — she paused and looked around at each of us — "I don't want to do Color Guard. I want to stay in Cheer."

It felt like ice water was running through my body. "You . . . what?"

She nodded. "I really like it. And also, I'm a leader in the squad now, so leaving would let those guys down." She turned to look straight at me. "As a leader yourself, I figure you might understand."

"Well, I don't! Not at all!" All the frustration and anger and hurt feelings I'd been holding on to since yesterday were exploding like hot kernels of popcorn. "Plus, I don't think that makes you a leader. I think that makes you a . . . a . . . a big traitor!"

"It does not, Dawn!" Now Darby was frowning at me. "Delaney doing what she wants doesn't make her a traitor. And guess what? I don't want to do Color Guard, either. I want to join photography."

"What's wrong with the two of you?" I said. "We waited so long and now finally there are three openings — finally we can all be together in Color Guard! What happened to all for one and one for all? What happened to sisterhood? You guys are just being selfish!"

"How are we being selfish?" Delaney asked. "You're the only one who wants to do Color Guard! How is it fair that we have to do what you want to do and you don't have to do the things we want to do?"

"What are you talking about? You like Color Guard!" I said.

Delaney shrugged. "It's okay. But I like cheerleading better. I can move more and be loud."

"And I like photography better," Darby said.

I shook my head over and over, as if I could erase everything in front of me. "I don't believe this!" I said. "You guys are just trying to undermine all my efforts, aren't you? You've turned against me for no reason. After all I've done!"

"Lately what you've done for me is get me in trouble for cheering the wrong events!" Delaney said.

"And thanks to you, I have detention after school. *Detention!*" Darby threw up her hands. "I never had detention before — ever!"

We were really yelling now. Somehow we'd forgotten where we were and who else was around.

"Yeah? Well, if you'd just go to class and speak up, I wouldn't have to go in your place pretending to be you, and neither would Delaney!"

For a moment, I had no idea why Delaney's eyes grew huge and Darby's head hung in shame. Then I realized what I'd just said.

"Ahem." Mr. Plunkett stood up on the other side of his desk and frowned down at us. "It seems to me that we have quite a bit to discuss."

CHAPTER THIRTY-ONE

High Treason

Darby

The only good thing about our talk with Mr. Plunkett was that he said to not worry about showing up for detention today, in light of this new information. Of course, that probably meant a worse fate was in store later, for all three of us. We were actual offenders now — our crimes being impersonating a sister, skipping class, impeding a couple of school competitions, and accidentally feeding school property to a goat.

Just like on our way to school that day, Dawn, Delaney, and I didn't talk on the walk home. We were still sore at one another. But I imagine, like me, they were also worried about how we were going to break our bad news to Mom. I'd never been a delinquent before, so I had no idea how young hooligans usually told their mothers about getting in trouble at school.

"Hello, girls," said a voice as we walked through the front

door. Only it wasn't Mom. Dad was sitting in an armchair across from Mom in the living room.

"Dad!" Delaney bounced over to him. "What are you doing here?"

"Lily called and asked me to come over."

Dawn glanced around, confused. "Lily did? I thought she was on vacation."

"I know," he said. "But she told me she'd be back here soon and that there was something she wanted to tell us all."

"Oh. Good. Because" — I glanced over at Dawn and Delaney — "we have something we want to tell you, too."

Dawn made big warning eyes at me — meaning she didn't think I should have said anything. I held her stare and raised my eyebrows — reminding her without words that we needed to tell them sometime anyway. It probably seems strange that we could have that conversation without talking, but we do it all the time. It's a triplet thing. Or maybe just a sister thing.

Just then I heard the sound of feet on our porch. I figured it was probably Lily, but soon came a familiar rap on our door. Sure enough, when I opened it up, there stood Aunt Jane, grinning one of her wide, warm smiles.

"Aunt Jane!" I shouted, and soon Dawn and Delaney were zooming up beside me. We each had a turn hugging her as she made her way inside. And Quincy also bounded over to greet her.

"Jane!" Dad said.

"Phil-dog!" Aunt Jane said.

And the two of them did that thing they always do where they pretend to have a boxing match and then end up hugging — while Mom stands off to the side shaking her head and rolling her eyes, but smiling, too.

"Don't tell me," Mom said as she stepped in for her hug, "did you also get a call from Lily?"

"I did," Aunt Jane said. "She told me to come as soon as I could. That it was important. What's it all about?"

Mom shrugged. "No idea."

"Aunt Jane showing up is a nice surprise no matter what!" Delaney said with a little happy dance.

For a moment, Dawn, Delaney, and I forgot about our problems and hurt feelings. Finding both Dad and Aunt Jane at the house felt like Christmas in September. We were standing in the foyer, listening to Aunt Jane talk about her new job running a campground as she played tug-of-war with Quincy, when the door opened suddenly and Lily and Alex walked in.

Again we went through our round of happy greetings, with Delaney bouncing and Quincy leaping about.

"Can, um . . . can everyone sit down for a sec?" Lily asked after a minute. Her face was carnation pink and there were squiggly worry lines on her forehead.

My eyes darted around to each of my other sisters. They seemed just as uneasy as I felt. Even Mom had that look she gets whenever we bring one of our official proposals to her — kind of worried and super alert all at once.

Lily and Alex sat on the couch with Aunt Jane, and Mom and Dad took the armchairs. I sat cross-legged on the carpet with Dawn and Delaney, between the armchairs and directly across from Lily.

"Good. Thanks for being here, everyone," Lily said. She seemed kind of winded, as if she'd been running a race — even though I knew she hadn't.

"What's up, sweetheart?" Aunt Jane said, giving Lily a bolstering smile.

Lily took a deep breath. "Alex and I . . ." She glanced over at him and he put his arm around her. "Alex and I got married."

Delaney raised her hand. "You mean you're *going to* get married."

"No," Alex said, "we already got married. See?" He lifted Lily's left hand. The white-gold engagement ring with the diamond and the two blue sapphires sparkled on her ring finger, and below it was a matching white-gold band.

Mom shook her head. "Wait . . . what?"

"Where?" Dad asked. "When?"

"How'd this happen?" Aunt Jane leaned forward, inspecting the ring.

"Alex joined me in New Orleans while I was visiting Clare," Lily said, "and, well, we eloped."

"Eloped?" Mom repeated. She and Dad exchanged shocked expressions.

"So . . . you won't have a wedding here?" I asked.

"Or anywhere?" Delaney asked.

"And you won't need our help?" Dawn asked. On the word *help*, her voice cracked.

Lily looked over at Alex, then at us. "No. It's all done. No need for a wedding."

Dawn got to her feet. "How could you do that?" she said, then turned and bolted out the front door.

"No!" Delaney said. "It's not fair!" Then she, too, ran out the door.

I couldn't say anything. I had so many thoughts in my head, and it was like they were shoving one another out of the way, making me unable to focus on any of them. Everything was ruined now. We wouldn't get to help Lily after all. No shower and no wedding. We wouldn't get to toss real flowers or make a toast or see Lily and Alex kiss after Reverend Hoffmeyer pronounced them husband and wife.

We weren't needed. We weren't wanted.

Tears were starting to fall from my eyes, so I stood and rushed out the door after my sisters. Delaney was already jogging laps, and Dawn was hiding in a spot on the porch between the wall and Quincy's crate. I ran over to the big pecan tree in the front yard and started climbing it. It was the best way I knew to get away from all the sad or scary stuff and clear my head.

I'd scrambled up that tree for years, and knew all the handholds, footholds, and strong limbs. I could do it without thinking about it. But maybe I'd grown too big for some of the grips and ledges, or maybe I was more upset than usual and not paying close enough attention.

Because the next thing I knew, there was a *whoosh* and a *snap* and suddenly, instead of sitting on a big limb, I was dangling by both hands from a branch.

A skinny branch. With no other limb in reach.

And even though my hands had a good grip, I knew they couldn't hang on for much longer.

I was going to fall.

CHAPTER THIRTY-TWO

Reinforcements

Delaney

Everything was awful. Everything was wrong and weird and terrible.

Those were the thoughts going around and around in my mind as I jogged around and around the yard. Tears were dripping everywhere, and at one point I had to stop, dig a tissue out of my pocket, and blow my nose. While I was doing that, something fell on my head.

"*Ow!*" I cried. I glanced down to see what it was and saw it was a white sandal.

That's when I looked up and saw her — Darby, hanging from a skinny little branch.

"Help," she said, kind of breathlessly.

"Oh! Oh! Oh no no no no no!" For a second I just started running in a smaller circle. I was so fearful, I had no idea what to do. Darby needed help — real help — and fast.

And so I did the one thing I've always been able to do in these situations. I threw back my head and screamed the most intolerably loud scream I've ever let out in my life. It was the kind of screaming that was powered not just by air inside my lungs but by panic and terror and love for my sister. And I kept on screaming until I saw Mom, Dad, Aunt Jane, Lily, Alex, Mr. and Mrs. Neighbor, and Ms. Woolcott come out of their houses and run toward us. Dawn told me later that the birds even stopped singing and the wind stopped blowing and a couple of cars pulled over on the nearby road.

As they raced over and saw what was going on, the grown-ups all started talking at once.

"Oh my goodness! What happened?"

"Darby — don't move!"

"That branch! It could break at any moment!"

"Someone do something!"

"Do we have a ladder that high? Anyone have a ladder that high?"

"I might. I'll go get mine."

"Would a ladder even help? We don't want her to fall on a hard ladder."

As they talked and shouted, I ran in a circle whimpering, wanting someone to do *something*. Mr. Neighbor was running to his toolshed for a ladder, but other than that, we were all just standing there, staring up at Darby's feet.

Then suddenly I heard a voice — loud and brash as if coming over a speaker.

"Listen! Listen to me!" It was Dawn, talking through the megaphone. She must have run and gotten it while everyone was yapping.

"Ms. Woolcott, call 911," she said. Ms. Woolcott nodded, pulled her phone out of her pocket, and started pressing buttons.

"Everyone else, we need something soft for her to land on."

"My mattress!" Mom said.

"Go! Everyone, go help Mom bring out the mattress." And off everyone went, lickety-split, except for me, Dawn, Ms. Woolcott on her phone, Mr. Neighbor running to get his ladder, and Dad.

"Dad, you should go, too!" I said to him. I was so upset, I was shaking and hopping at the same time, so my words came out twittery and broken.

"No, I'm staying here. They have enough people," Dad said, staring up at Darby's feet. "I'm going to stand right beneath her, so if she drops, I'll break her fall."

"But you'll get hurt, too!" I wailed.

"I don't care." His eyes stayed on Darby. He looked so scared, like I've never seen before, and his words were so frightening that I almost started screaming again.

"The firefighters are on their way!" Ms. Woolcott said, lifting her hand with the phone in it.

"Hang on, Darby!" Dawn said through the megaphone. "Don't worry. Help is on the way!"

"I don't know if I can," came Darby's trembly voice. "My hands are getting slippery."

Just then, I heard a clatter and looked toward our porch in time to see Mrs. Neighbor holding open the door so that Mom, Alex, Lily, and Aunt Jane could maneuver out her queen-sized mattress. I had so many thoughts and felt so many emotions all at once. I was impatient and wanted them to hurry. I was terrified for Darby and Dad. I was mad that I couldn't just sprout wings, fly into the air, and help my sister down from the tree. And I was remembering all the times I secretly jumped up and down on Mom's pillow-top mattress, marveling at how soft and strong it was.

I hoped it still was.

As soon as they made it down the steps, they carried it over to the tree faster than I would have expected.

Mom shouted, "Phil!" and Dad moved out of the way.

After a little bit of back and forth, they set down the mattress and stepped back. I could feel myself breathe again — and I wondered how long I'd been holding it. I could hear sirens in the distance, coming closer.

"Will that help?" Mom asked. Her voice was just as jagged as Dad's had been.

"Sure it will," Aunt Jane said, sounding reassuring. "We just need to make sure she doesn't bounce off."

"Let's gather round the mattress, everyone!" came Dawn's voice through the megaphone. "Gather round and stop her from bouncing off onto the ground."

Dawn dropped the megaphone and joined us as we circled the mattress, holding up our hands, shield-like, the way Aunt Jane was doing.

"I'm going to fall!" Darby said. "I'm sorry! I can't hold it! I'm going to . . . *Aaaugh!*"

The next thing I knew, Darby was whirring past. She hit the mattress, bounced up, hit it again, and mainly stayed put. It didn't even seem like my sister. More like a sister-sized rag doll. I have no idea if she bounced into anyone or not, but we were all still standing. For a moment, it was quiet. Just the sirens in the distance. Then Darby made a sound, kind of a squeak.

"Darby, sweetie. Are you okay?" Mom started to climb onto the mattress, but Aunt Jane held her back.

"Wait now," she said. "Everyone wait. Let's not touch her. She could have injuries."

"I think I'm okay," Darby said, stirring slightly. Her eyes blinked and a weird smile came over her. "That was kinda neat."

"Dagnabbit, Darby!" Dawn hollered. She was full-on crying, like she hadn't done in front of us for years. "Don't ever do that again! I love you, you wild, pigheaded daredevil!"

The firefighters were pulling up now. A short red truck stopped in our driveway and people jumped out. As they rushed toward us, I heard Darby say, "I won't, Dawn. Not ever again. I promise. And I love you, too."

"And I love all of you!" I shouted. "And I love that we all love each other!"

It was the best kind of cheering, for all the best reasons.

CHAPTER THIRTY-THREE

Disaster Relief

Dawn

It naturally took a while for the hubbub to die down. The first responders determined that Darby was fine — no broken bones, concussion, or other injuries. Just a severe case of foolhardiness. They warned she would likely be sore the next few days, told Mom and Dad about some painkillers she could take and what to look out for. After that, they climbed into their truck and drove away.

The Neighbors and Ms. Woolcott stuck around long enough to hear Darby pronounced *reckless but fine*, and then Mr. Neighbor said to Ms. Woolcott, "Come on, Josephine. Let's let this family have some time to themselves."

Ms. Woolcott was sniffling and dabbing her eyes with a flowered handkerchief. It almost seemed like she didn't want to go, but then Mrs. Neighbor invited her over for iced tea and homemade muffins, and the three of them walked across the street to the Neighbors' cozy front porch, Mr.

Neighbor carrying his ladder and Mrs. Neighbor patting Ms. Woolcott's back.

Ms. Woolcott wasn't the only one crying. Mom, Dad, Lily, Aunt Jane, Delaney, and I were all either boohooing loudly or regularly wiping tears off our cheeks and blowing our noses. Aunt Jane told us later that when your body fills with strong emotion — the way it did when Darby was in peril — it has to be let out some way, and crying is really a good way.

"I'm sorry," Darby kept saying as she sobbed. "I didn't mean to." Even as Mom and Dad reassured her that it was okay, she kept saying she was sorry. When they brought the mattress back in and found a few ants on it, she cried and apologized for that. She even apologized for a mosquito bite Alex got.

Finally everything was back where it should be, and we all gathered in the living room again — where we'd been before the big calamity.

"I feel like this mess all started with me," Lily said. "Everyone got so upset at our news."

"It's not your fault," Darby said. "And we're happy for you guys — really. We were just . . . just . . ."

"We were just surprised," Delaney finished for her.

"And a little let down," I added. "But only because we'd wanted to be there."

"I know. I'm sorry. But I just couldn't go through with a wedding," Lily said, her eyes focused on the floor. Alex sat beside her, holding her hand. "Every time I started to even think about invitations or catering or picking out formal wear, I'd feel sick to my stomach."

"I know," Delaney said, patting Lily's and Alex's clasped hands. "I hate fancy clothes, too."

"When Clare invited me to visit," Lily went on, "I just thought, *Why not do it there?* Alex could join me, my best friend would already be there, and we'd be in the beautiful French Quarter of New Orleans." She paused and closed her eyes. "I thought, *Let's just get it over with.* So I asked Alex."

"And I told her, if that's what she wanted, then that's what I wanted," Alex said. "It didn't matter to me where it took place or who was there. To me, the only important detail was that she be my bride."

Lily smiled at him — the biggest, happiest, sparkliest smile I've ever seen. He leaned over and kissed her cheek.

"I hope you'll eventually understand." Lily glanced around at me, Darby, and Delaney. "To us, it's the marriage that matters, not the wedding. But I am very sorry if our decision hurt y'all's feelings."

"Honey, we are so happy for you two," Mom said. "We really are."

"We were just caught off guard, is all," Dad said.

"Aw heck. I for one am pleased as punch," Aunt Jane said. "Now I don't have to put on a dress!"

We all chuckled at that.

"Do Alex's parents know?" Mom asked.

Alex nodded. "We stopped on the way here. We wanted to catch them before they went on their trip to the coast."

"I'm sorry I got upset," Darby said, more tears streaming down her cheeks. "I was just disappointed we didn't get to help. But I'm way way way more happy than I am disappointed."

"Plus, we've had a rough time of it since school started," Delaney added. "So a lot of that wailing and carrying-on had been kind of stored up inside us — and had nothing to do with you. We overreacted."

The two of them looked over at me. I got to my feet and turned to face Lily and Alex.

"I also apologize for my reaction," I said. I cleared my throat and tried to find the words to explain what I'd been thinking for the past hour or so. "You all might not realize this, but I'm a little bit stubborn. I tend to look into the future and make a picture in my mind of what I want to happen. Then, when it doesn't turn out that way, I can get riled up. But that's my problem. And I need to be not so set in my ways about how things are supposed to turn out. I'm . . . well . . . I'm working on that."

I glanced at Darby and Delaney to see if they realized I was apologizing to them, too. The warm smiles on their faces told me they did.

"Lily has it right, you know," I went on. "Sometimes you have to do what's right for you, despite what other people want. Even if it means letting people down or being separated from your sisters."

Mom stood up and put her arms around me. "I'm very proud of you girls," she said.

"Me too," Dad said, scooping Darby up in a sideways hug.

"Me three," Aunt Jane said, reaching over to muss up Delaney's hair. "You really came together when it mattered."

"Me four!" Lily said.

"Me five!" Alex said.

I felt a glow come over me. Only I couldn't tell if it was coming from inside me or from everyone around me. Maybe both.

"Thanks, everyone," I said, settling into the hug. "And Dad? Mom? I really hope you two hold on to those feelings of pride and love because, well, any minute now you're going to get a phone call from the school."

CHAPTER THIRTY-FOUR

Reparations

Darby

We got to school early the next day because we had so much to do. First, I handed my schedule-change sheet to Mrs. Delgado, the photography teacher. I asked Dawn and Delaney to wait in the hallway so I could talk to her myself — I needed the practice. Luckily she was really nice. "Pleased to meet you," she said to me. "I've heard a lot of good things about you from Wanda." It was great to hear, even if it did make me turn red and talk in a too-soft voice for a while.

Next, we all went to Coach Manbeck's office so that Dawn and I could hand in our schedule-change notices to her, too. Plus, Dawn had to return the megaphone.

"Thank you for letting me borrow it," Dawn said, handing it over. Her fingers stayed on it as Coach Manbeck pulled it away, creating a small squeaking sound, and I noticed how she kept on gazing at it longingly.

"You're welcome," Coach Manbeck said.

"Also . . . I apologize for all those times you were summoned to Mr. Plunkett's office on account of our bonus cheering," Dawn said.

"Thanks for saying that," Coach Manbeck said. "I know you just wanted to help."

"True, but it was poor planning on my part," Dawn said. "I didn't understand that you can't make someone accept help."

Delaney nodded. "You should wait until asked."

"Or until they're in mortal danger," I added.

"I still think the school could pay more attention to other sports, but maybe a raucous pep squad is not what they need," Dawn said. "If I come up with a better idea, I'll run it by you, okay?"

Coach Manbeck grinned at her. "I'd appreciate that."

Coach said she was sorry to see me and Dawn go, and she wished us good luck in photography and Color Guard.

Since Color Guard was busy practicing for an upcoming game, we next visited Mrs. Champion. We found her at her desk, reading a newspaper.

"Hi, Mrs. Champion," I said.

"Hi, girls," she said. "Mr. Plunkett filled me in on your strategy to fool us in order to help Darby." Her expression was pointed but not mean. Even so, my shame felt heavier. I was amazed I could stay upright.

"Mrs. Champion, we have something we need to say to you." My voice was a little shaky, so I paused to swallow and take a breath. "My sisters and I — we're all very sorry. We shouldn't have done those switcheroos. It was unethical and disrespectful to you, and it cheated me out of learning."

"Thank you. I guess it ended up being a learning experience after all, huh? Maybe more than you bargained for?"

"It was a learning experience for all three of us," Dawn said.

"Maybe even more," Delaney said.

"Darby, I am sorry that you were so uneasy with my method of assessment. And I'm sorry you didn't feel you could come tell me about it."

I couldn't look at her. Instead, I stared down at the tips of my sneakers. "I should have. I was just embarrassed."

"Well, perhaps I should have anticipated that some students wouldn't be as comfortable with such a grading situation. I'm used to students who love talking and try to talk as much as they can. I guess because that's how I am."

"And me," Delaney said.

"And me," Dawn said.

"So I've witnessed," Mrs. Champion said with a knowing grin. "I tell you what, Darby. You're the first to hear this, but I'll be announcing a change in my grading policy next week. As long as students demonstrate knowledge of the subject in some way — via written paragraphs or class discussion — their daily grade will be passing. Think you can do that?"

"I can," I said, making myself look at her. "In fact . . . can I also use visuals? I've been taking pictures around town and a lot of them are about history — Texas history, local history, even my history. Could I make a slide show and present it to the class? The thing is, I need to try to not be shy, and I think doing this will help."

"That would work out nicely, Darby. Thanks." Mrs. Champion turned toward Dawn and Delaney. "And as for you two . . ."

I could see Dawn gulp, and Delaney went, "Uh-oh."

"If you would like to use your speaking skills in a more productive way, I teach speech/debate here at school, with competitions throughout the year. Perhaps you would like to join us?"

"I've already committed to Cheer and Dawn is joining Color Guard," Delaney said.

"Hold up." Dawn was tapping her chin with her index finger. "The thing is," she said, "Color Guard just doesn't seem as much fun without you guys in it. It was an all-for-one activity."

She turned to Mrs. Champion. "So you say in your class I'd be making speeches?"

"That's right."

"Are there megaphones?"

"Not usually, but we sometimes use microphones."

Dawn stood there for a moment, brow furrowed, finger tapping. Finally she held out her hand to Mrs. Champion. "Count me in."

CHAPTER THIRTY-FIVE

Jamboree

Delaney

Where should we stand, Delaney?" Aurelia asked. She stood with her arms behind her back, pom-poms in both hands, and it made her look like she had a big silvery rabbit's tail. I started to laugh a little; then I started wondering what Mynah would look like with a silver pom-pom tail. Finally I snapped back to attention. This was a special day — perhaps the most special our family has had so far — and I had an important job to do.

"I think you guys are already in a good place," I said. "Just tell the rest of the Pom Squad to watch out for ants."

"Okay. How long until we start?"

"Any minute now."

I was so nervous, my usual bouncing didn't help, so I kept doing my cheer jumps. So far I loved being a cheerleader. I loved being able to jump and shout and get all the pent-up energy out of me. But I also loved feeling the energy build in a crowd — like we were conducting an excitement sym-phony. I'd never thought I'd find something that lets me leap around and be noisy.

"Here they come!" Darby and Wanda came running from their lookout posts in the driveway. I craned my neck to peek. Sure enough, there was Lily's white Honda coming down the road.

"Places, people!" Dawn trumpeted. "This is not a drill. Repeat, this is not a drill!"

Everyone quickly shuffled around to make sure they were out of view, either behind the house or a tree or the rabbit hutch. We stood hunched and ready, waiting for the signal. My knees were bouncing and my closed mouth was making a high-pitched squeal, like a boiling teapot.

Dawn, reunited with a borrowed cheer megaphone just for this event, peered around the corner of the porch. There came the sound of tires crunching down our gravel drive, then a pause, and then the slam of a car door. Dawn raised the megaphone to her lips, shouting, "Aaaaand go!"

That was our cue. The three drummers who showed up started a lively beat, and I led the cheerleaders around the corner to the front of the house, whooping and hollering the whole way. Behind us came all the assembled guests, also cheering. Some clapped and others used various noisemakers.

Lily and Alex froze in place, their eyes huge with surprise.

"Why do I have a feeling you three are behind this?" Alex said as I reached him. A huge smile took up the bottom half of his face.

"What on earth is going on?" Lily asked, also grinning.

"Instead of a shower, we're throwing you a marriage pep rally!" I said.

"A special gathering to commemorate your happy nuptials," Darby said.

"We wanted to boost your spirit and encourage you to do your best in the marriage!" Dawn said, and we *yay*ed and *hurrah*ed some more.

Next, Dawn and Darby led Lily and Alex behind the house to two chairs all decorated with streamers, where they could sit and watch the rally. Mom, Dad, Aunt Jane, and all the other guests gathered behind them.

As soon as I gave them a nod, the drum line started pounding out an irresistible rhythm — *Bomp! Tap! Bompbomp! Tap!* — and the Pom Squad waved their silver pom-poms while the other cheerleaders and I led everyone in spelling Lily's and Alex's names. After that, we did some standard cheers that we'd changed up to relate to the occasion, like *"Let's* (clap) *get* (clap) *a little bit married, M-A-R-R-I-E-D!"* and *"Love can't be beat!"* But my favorite was one I came up with myself that went:

First you get a ring.
Then you get down on one knee.
Then you say, "I do,"

And it's love eternally!

Marriage! Marriage! Go-o-o-o, Marriage!

It was splendiferous. In between cheers and jumps, I'd take in the scene. Everywhere I looked was the smiling face of a family member or neighbor or good friend. Colorful streamers had been strung around trees and porch railings, and spirit banners were hung against the wall of the back porch and on the rabbit hutch, congratulating Lily and Alex and cheering for love. On all the tables were scatterings of confetti and mason jars full of freshly picked flowers from Ms. Woolcott's yard.

But the best sight of all was Alex and Lily holding hands and laughing and smiling as they sat in their special chairs.

Before long, it was time for our big finish. The cheerleaders stepped forward, chanting, "Kiss! Kiss! Kiss! Kiss!" And all the rest of the guests joined in, circling the happy couple from other directions. We chanted faster and louder until finally Alex and Lily turned to each other and started kissing. Once again we cheered, clapped, jumped, shook pom-poms, and drummed.

When it was over, we turned on some music and everyone milled around talking and eating. Aunt Jane served up her famous chili, one pot with meat and another vegetarian — both made even more delectable by the Neighbors' homemade corn muffins. And Mom brought out five big pans of peach cobbler she baked, which most people topped with the vanilla ice cream Dad brought.

We had told the Cheer Squad and drummers that they didn't have to hang around after the initial cheers and chants, but most of them did anyway, and there was plenty of food. "This is even better than the pep rallies at school!" Lynette said between bites of cobbler.

I grabbed a bowl of chili and a muffin and joined the crowd around Lily and Alex.

"Well, this is the *second* time I wasn't able to see you get married," Ms. Woolcott was saying to Lily. "But I have to say, this party is ab-so-LUTE-ly perfect. And I'm so happy for the two of you." She pulled out the flowered hankie again and dabbed at her eyes.

"Did you enjoy the rally?" I asked Alex as Lily comforted Ms. Woolcott.

"Who needs a big wedding when you can have this? A marriage pep rally is a fantastic idea."

"It's a spirit boost!" I said with a bounce. "So are you ready to win?"

He laughed. "Well, I'm already married to Lily, so I already feel like I've won."

Just then Mr. and Mrs. Neighbor came up to congratulate Alex and Lily. I stepped back so they'd have room to hug.

"Well done, you," said a familiar voice. I turned to see Aunt Jane smiling at me. "Lily wasn't up for a wedding, and I understand and respect that. But this was a real nice way of showing them how happy we are for them."

"Thanks, Aunt Jane." As she tossed her arm around me

and pulled me close, I was careful not to get chili on her blouse. It was nice having her around this past week. She'd hung around to help Lily pack up and move out, but she helped us a lot, too. In addition to helping us brainstorm ideas for the marriage pep rally, she also helped us set up our new beds at Dad's house while she was over for some of his famous burgers. It was funny — in a good way — that Aunt Jane was able to visit more often just as Lily was moving out. It's like everyone in my life was still there, only rearranged.

Just then I spotted Bree in the crowd. She was wearing a black dress and red cowboy boots and a big happy grin. "That was splendid," she said.

"I didn't see you get here. I'm glad you got time off."

"Are you kidding? I needed to see this for myself," she said. "This love story has been one epic adventure. So whose idea was the rally? Yours?"

I thought for a moment. "It was either me, Dawn, or Darby. I can't remember which."

"Well, that narrows it down," Bree said, her smile sliding sideways. "I swear sometimes it's like you three are all one person."

"Yeah, but we're not," I said.

Even though Dawn, Darby, and I did a lot together, and often thought alike — so much so that we often couldn't remember whose idea was whose — we were also starting to do different things and hang out with different people. And that was okay. We were all going to be okay.

As I glanced out over the crowd, I spied Dawn, learning a chess move from Lucas. Darby and Wanda were walking all around taking photographs, occasionally pausing to show each other the pics they'd taken so far. Later, Darby would take a break from documenting the event to join Lucas for a lasso demonstration. Meanwhile, I had plans to show off Mynah to my cheer pals.

But as the party went on, every now and then one of us glanced up, caught the eye of another triplet, and grinned — and we knew what that grin meant and what that sister felt, no matter how far away we were.

It was happiness all around.

CHAPTER THIRTY-SIX

And Crown Thy Good with Sisterhood

Dawn

I sat inside Forever's sipping ice water and waiting for Darby and Delaney to show up before ordering pie. I had come early to grab a good table before the evening rush, and luckily I nabbed our favorite spot — the small white round one right next to the window.

As I kept a lookout, I thought about the events of the past couple of weeks. After our week of after-school detention was over, we were able to plan some after-school fun. Last Friday, Delaney and the other newly minted seventh-grade cheerleaders had met with the eighth-grade cheerleaders at Cherry's house for an unofficial welcome party. Delaney had come back all smiles, with navy and silver ribbons braided into her hair. But she had apparently used up so much of her bounce and chatter, she was practically Darby-like the rest of the evening.

Darby had spent the past several days learning more photography tips from Wanda so she could get caught up with the rest of the class. I've noticed a teensy change in her, too. At school she's already been more likely to approach people she doesn't know and talk to them — if only to ask to take their picture.

Meanwhile, I spent most of today with Lucas. I headed to his house after church and apologized again for the whole chess debacle. He was a good sport about it and said he understood; then he invited me in for Parcheesi and bagels. While we played (we each won a game), he admitted that he'd seen me practicing in debate class, having peeked in while working as office aide. He had some good tips, too, like not to cross my arms and tap my foot while my opponent was talking. He also said he liked my habit of tapping my chin, calling it cute. Then he turned the same color as the strawberry cream cheese.

I like that he came to watch me in action and then shared honest advice. It's something Darby and Delaney would do, only it seemed — I don't know — sweeter, somehow, coming from him. I guess I never realized that some of the support and understanding I got from my sisters, I could get from good friends, too.

I've come to understand a lot of new things. For example, I used to think being a triplet meant that you did everything together — or at least as many things as possible. Now I'm starting to think what it really means is that you're always there for one another. It's tough to explain. I guess an analogy might be that instead of being stuck in the tree together, we're below, making sure everyone has a soft landing.

Just when I was starting to get impatient, I could see Darby out the window, tootling up the road with a camera around her neck. As usual, her gaze was wandering all over. When she was just a few yards away from Ever's, I caught sight of a colorful streak off to the right. Soon after, Delaney zoomed into view. She jogged up beside Darby, pacing all around her and chattering nonstop. She continued jabbering all the way up the steps and through the door.

". . . so I asked Coach Manbeck if Mynah could be part of the rally, kind of like a mascot, but she said no and . . . Oh, there's Dawn. Dawn!" Delaney hopped up and down a couple of times. "We're here!"

"I brought a notebook and pen to take notes," Darby said.

"Excellent," I said. "I think we should probably get our food first — before it gets busy."

"And before they run out of chocolate pie," Delaney added.

Leaving behind our papers and pens to mark our spot, we all went up to the counter to peruse the day's desserts. I ordered a slice of apple pie with a scoop of ice cream. Delaney — of course — got a slice of chocolate chess pie with whipped cream, and after lots of deliberation, Darby got a slice of lemon meringue pie. After a moment or two of silent eating — well, except for all the *mmm*s — I figured it was time to get down to business.

I cleared my throat to get their attention. I'm not exactly sure why, but I felt a little nervous.

"Here are the agendas I printed out," I said, passing out two extra copies of the sheet of paper in front of me. "But first, I was wondering, should we continue to have meetings? I mean, should we still organize them like this, with voting and keeping minutes and such?" I tried to keep my voice from sounding shaky. I managed to do it, but I did lose volume at the end of my last sentence.

Darby and Delaney looked at each other, then back at me.

"Why would we stop?" Delaney asked.

"Yeah," Darby said. "I like our meetings."

I smiled one of those smiles where not only do the corners of your mouth lift, but your whole body, heart, and soul rise up a little. "Very well," I said. "Then I propose that, since school and other activities keep us so busy during the week, we reserve this time — Sunday afternoons — for us to gather here for pie and official business."

"I second that," Darby said.

"I third it," Delaney said, and we all clinked our forks together in a formal gesture of support.

"After all," Delaney said between bites of chocolate chess pie, "it's the triplet thing to do."

"It's the Brewster thing to do," Darby added.

"And it's the right thing to do," I said.

Darby lifted her hand in a *halt* gesture. "Only there's a problem," she said. "This decision isn't official yet because you haven't called the meeting to order."

"She's right, you know," Delaney said.

"Very well," I said and lightly pounded my fist on the table. "I call this meeting to order."

ACKNOWLEDGMENTS

This series is so lucky to have a wise and supportive family at Scholastic. Erin Black, you know this world and these characters as if you live among them. Thank you for all the care you've shown to me and the Brewsters. Thanks also to David Levithan, Melissa Schirmer, Yaffa Jaskoll, Michelle Campbell, Lizette Serrano, Emily Heddleson, and Brooke Shearouse.

During the writing of this book, I received invaluable help from Cynthia Leitich Smith, Nikki Loftin, Andrew Barton, Michael Alves, Carolyn Dee Flores, Divya Srinivasan, Amanda Ford, and Esther Ford. Also, the heart of this story arose from a conversation with my good friend Clare Dunkle — one of the wisest people I know. Thank you, all of you. I am truly blessed to have you in my life.

To Erin Murphy and my EMLA community: a huge,

glittery, unicorn-and-rocket-cat thank-you. When the writing gets tough, I persevere so I can keep earning my place among you.

I am deeply grateful to all of the readers who wrote to say thanks and suggest ideas. Please keep reading books and keep on being you. I'd also like to acknowledge the educators who work so hard to create readers, writers, and book-lovers. You are true heroes.

Lastly but forever-ly, thank you to Chris, for reading, listening, and always believing.

ABOUT THE AUTHOR

Like the Brewster triplets, Jennifer Ziegler is a native Texan and a lover of family, history, art, loyal dogs, and homemade pie. When she was a student, she tried various activities until she found what suited her best: writing for school publications and serving as a library aide. And although she never got in serious trouble, she was caught daydreaming quite often. Jennifer is the author of *Revenge of the Flower Girls*, *Revenge of the Angels*, and *Revenge of the Happy Campers*, as well as books for older readers, including *Sass & Serendipity* and *How Not to Be Popular*. She lives in Austin, Texas, with her husband, author Chris Barton, and their four children.